BLACK OPS: ZULU

TOM STILES THRILLERS BOOK 1

ARTHUR BOZIKAS

Copyright (C) 2021 Arthur Bozikas

Layout design and Copyright (C) 2021 by Next Chapter

Published 2021 by Terminal Velocity – A Next Chapter Imprint

Edited by Fading Street Services

Cover art by CoverMint

This book is a work of fiction. Names, characters, places, and incidents are the product of the author's imagination or are used fictitiously. Any resemblance to actual events, locales, or persons, living or dead, is purely coincidental.

All rights reserved. No part of this book may be reproduced or transmitted in any form or by any means, electronic or mechanical, including photocopying, recording, or by any information storage and retrieval system, without the author's permission.

ALSO BY ARTHUR BOZIKAS

The Book Glasses

ACKNOWLEDGMENTS

I would like to thank those who helped to make this novel possible. Thanks to my wife Helen, and our children Jimmy and Pamela for their dedicated love and support, and to both of our parents and to all of our immediate family for their tireless affections.

As a final point, I'd like to dedicate this novel to all the past, present and future blood donors for their precious generosity. I like to consider myself an action writer, but their action has and will always continue to save lives all around the world. I consider them all to be the true action heroes!

Arthur

1

Lightning speared through the worn blinds of the Motel Voyager. Tom Stiles fastened his Jaeger-LeCoultre around his wrist, his face pulsing between light and dark. Rain plunged down outside.

"Natasha, summer's over," Tom said, without turning from the storm outside.

"I'm glad; I hate the heat."

Tom looked over the grey-brown carpet and followed the trail of hat, dress, bra, and stockings to the bed. She lay beneath the sheets with her arm stroking the pillow which still retained the impression of his head.

"It means I have to go now."

Natasha turned to the bedside table, unclipped a cigarette from her diamond-studded cigarette case and lit it. "So, I was just your seasonal lover, is that it?"

"You are more than that, Tash, but we knew this day was coming."

"Save me the, 'it's not you, I still love my wife' speech!"

"I have to return to my daughters."

"Don't give me that, Tom. Don't tell me you have to leave;

you're volunteering to leave. You could take me with you … At least stay one more night. Come back to bed."

Tom did not turn around, but he could see her reflection in the mirror. She had pushed aside the sheet covering her body. He closed his eyes. He knew that one more glimpse of her thigh, or her silhouette against the crumpled pink sheets would weaken his resolve. Taking a sip from his hip flask, he picked up his heavy firefighting boots and walked out the door. He heard a glass shatter on the door behind him.

Tom ran through the dark car park, hunched against the storm. His black BMW was parked next to Natasha's dark green convertible with the number plate MG 1979. He turned the key in the ignition and the radio started up; the 3:00 a.m. news was just beginning.

Tom thought he should sit through the rain. He turned on his mobile. Fifteen missed calls, all from Victoria. Well, what did he expect? He had been due home hours ago. Garth Brooks began singing *Thunder Rolls*, and Tom pulled out onto the Great Western Highway.

The city's silhouette throbbed in the distance, but the road ahead was devoid of taillights. Now and again a truck passed in the opposite direction. He came to a complete stop at the intersection in front of a red light and glanced at the clock—three forty-five. He exhaled for what seemed like the first time that summer. *Home soon*, he thought. Another summer of fighting fires was over; another few houses saved; some scares but no death, no scars, and no harm done … excluding the harm he had done to Natasha. He thought of her lying naked beneath him again and let the thought go. Home soon.

He exhaled again and asked himself if he really did still love Victoria. He had imagined taking Natasha home with him but that was not possible. Yes, he had contemplated it but knew it would destroy Victoria. And it was far too soon after the death of their mother to turn his daughters' lives upside down again. The girls were still grieving, as he was, and they had become accustomed to Victoria being around.

He had lost his parents when he was a child, and that pain defined him. There had been other women after his wife Helen's death, women he had found every summer when he volunteered. He would search them for any resemblance to Helen and judge them against what was now becoming a faded, idealised image of her. But Natasha? He was falling in love with Natasha for the way she smoked a cigarette, the slight Russian accent that became more prominent when she swore, and her indefatigable body.

He struggled then, as he always had, to make some connection between all these things. The death of his wife, the death of his parents and his brother … they were like withered bouquets left by the side of the road. The long tuneless white noise of death had followed him his entire life. He felt no sense of resolution; he often puzzled over an indistinct question that woke him, noiseless, always around midnight. But beside Natasha he slept at ease.

A sheet of what looked like lightning illuminated the entire crossroads and shocked Tom into pressing the brakes even harder as he waited for the lights to turn green. Tyres screeched behind him. Suddenly, his body jolted forward, and the air bag exploded in his face. Pain seared through him. And then there was no horizon lights, no road, no car, nothing except pain from his spine to his fingertips and a sense of helpless, unbidden flying as if he had entered a recurring dream. Then the car seemed to gather him back in. A wheel rolled past the driver side window. Then, darkness.

2

IN MEETING ROOM 811B OF THE AUSTRALIAN NATIONAL SECURITY Agency, Divisional Chief of Black Ops Paul Henderson and Commander Alexandria Tap were staring at a laptop. Rioting men wearing balaclavas and holding Molotov cocktails streamed across the screen. The men shouted and held up placards reading 'Free Carraldo'.

"Four Cuban judges were killed last month," Paul said.

"What are they protesting against?"

"The law."

"Chief, please drag to 2.12, pause, lift and magnify. Then zoom to under the burnt flag."

In the dark corner of the screen a man's face appeared, clean-shaven with one blue eye and one green eye. The man was old and walked with a walking stick and he wore a poncho over what looked to be a white shirt.

"His name is Cerberus, Chief. The dog that guarded the gates of hell. But the funny thing is we believe it is his real name?"

Paul stood, brushed down the lapels of his wool suit, and walked the length of the room. He paused and turned back. Commander Tap raised one long black eyebrow in anticipation. She had known him long enough to anticipate that his small stroll around the room would precede an announcement.

"Commander Tap. I think it is time to go for a more field-based solution, starting tomorrow. This guy comes out of the shadows and then disappears into the shadows again. We need someone on the ground."

"We'll need more Black Ops whizzes for the scheduled bang and burn jobs. So, do we have the budget for that, Paul?"

"Leave that to me. There's a partnership cooking with the big house on Pennsylvania Avenue. Seems they got intel that Cerberus is heading to Australia and they want him as badly as we do. If judges start appearing dead in this country …"

"Jesus, seriously, is there anything you can tell me right now?"

"I promise to tell you when I have all the details. All I know is the gods may have delivered us an option."

"Care to share?"

"The man we want is ex-Duntroon and did a stint in Afghanistan with our Special Operation Task Group. SOTG were tasked to provide security during a training validation exercise for the Provincial Response Company of Uruzgan (that's the PRC-U) in Tarin Kot, Afghanistan. SOTG have worked with PRC-U special police officers since 2001 and turned over operations in Uruzgan province in 2005."

"Did you know him from Duntroon?"

"I recall he came through the year I got this assignment. Bit of a public face now and he puts out fires, literally. Prior to that, he went to the States and worked for a subunit of the US Marines after six months at West Point to complete his Special Ops combat mustering. Actually, he did two trips through Afghanistan when the shit was at its heaviest. Then, when they were about to promote him, he asked to be transferred home. Said he wanted to start a business!"

3

Tom felt disembodied, fluid. The sides of the road had become blurred, and he faded in and out of consciousness. He turned and looked into the back seat and saw the faces of his dead wife, his dead parents, and his dead brother. They looked at him with pity. Helen whispered, "Can you hear me?"

A red light was approaching at speed, coming directly at him, sirens blaring. He lapsed out of consciousness and in his mind, he saw a leopard keeping pace with the car as he drove. He accelerated but the leopard stayed alongside, moving at an easy lope. He thought of his daughters, Sophia and Angela, just as his eyes were closing.

"Can you hear me?"

Tom woke wearing an oxygen mask with two tall figures beside him and the alarm in his car beeping incessantly. He was stretchered to an ambulance. Pain pulsed through his body and he could taste blood. He tested the movement in his extremities, and cautiously turned his neck left and right. *All in need of repair*, he thought, *but no parts missing*. He heard the paramedic say "rear-ended." He raised his hands—they were streaked with blood and the face of his watch was smashed. His wrist was bandaged, and his shirt had been cut off revealing the thin black armband around his left bicep.

As his breathing began to steady, two police vehicles pulled up. One of the paramedics informed the officers that the driver of the second vehicle had died, probably on impact, and that when the fire brigade had finished cleaning up around the vehicle, they could remove the body and begin their investigations.

Tom tried to sit up. He overheard a police officer calling in the details of the accident. "Driver of first vehicle, male Caucasian, alive, condition steady, internal injuries. Driver of second vehicle, female Caucasian, deceased."

"I'm Senior Constable Peter Collins. Are you alright, sir?' asked a police officer, as he took out his notebook.

"Yes ... yes ... I think I'm fine, officer," Tom replied.

"Can I see your licence, please?"

Tom slowly removed his wallet and handed it over.

"Okay, now can you tell me what happened?"

"I was just driving home, and next thing I knew I was on a gurney."

"So, what are you doing out here after four on a Wednesday morning?"

"I'm an SES volunteer just coming back from my last job, back burning, up around the Faulconbridge area."

The officer wrote the word *volunteer* in his notebook and leaned closer towards Tom to hear him better but also trying to shelter himself from the wind and rain.

"I was a volunteer, 2001 bushfires. Say you know, the heat the last few weeks ... thank God for this storm. Do you feel okay, Tom?"

Tom sat up a little and saw the green MG with its front demolished.

Natasha. Tow trucks and police cars surrounded the car. An ambulance drove off. Flashing blue, red, white, and orange lights lit up the area, pulsing in the rain. There was blood and glass on the bitumen. Steam rose from the side of the road. Then, from nowhere, a police helicopter lit up the entire area. Tom was blinded. He felt a needle go into his arm, and everything went black.

4

Tom arrived home after being stitched up and kept under observation for two hours. He had no broken bones and the lacerations were not deep. The doctor told him he was lucky to be alive and was surprised he was not in shock.

Tom put it down to being ex-army. After all, he had come through bloodbaths in Afghanistan hotspots. He had seen a man cut in half by a rocket launcher, and another who had stepped on a landmine and all they could bury of him was his head. But Tom was in shock. His lover was dead. He tried to fathom it—a few hours ago she was lying in his arms and now Natasha was dead.

It was daylight when he approached the front door and noticed all the lights both inside and outside the house were on. Tom stood on the jute doormat and wiped blood from his shoes over the word *agape*. He opened the door, entered, and clicked his fingers. The lights switched off and he found his twin daughters sitting at the top of the stairs basking in the morning sun. His partner, Victoria, hovered above them, looking as fierce as the huntress Diana.

"Fifteen calls, Tom. Why don't you answer your damn phone? I've been going out of my mind here. Oh, my God, what happened to you?"

"Calm down, Vic. You're frightening the girls."

"Oh my God," she repeated. "Your face is busted up … what … what happened?"

"I've been in a car accident. It's alright, I'm fine. Someone rear-ended me. Some bruised ribs and lacerations but I've been sewn up and sent home. I would have called but my head has been all over the place."

Dressed in their school uniforms, the twins look terrified. Victoria tried to kiss him, but he moved his face away. She ran to the kitchen, grabbed ice from the freezer, wrapped it up in a tea towel, and placed it gently on his bruised face.

5

After getting him comfortable in the lounge with the ice and a beaker full of Glenmorangie, Vic got Angela and Sophia to kiss him and then quickly walked them to Tom's in-laws next door for their routine drive to school.

All too soon, she returned. "Now, tell me everything. What the hell happened?"

Tom sipped his scotch and started his rehearsed speech. "After I spoke to you on the phone yesterday arvo, Bill, you know Bill, my SES volunteer area commander…"

"I know who Bill is!"

"Please, Vic, be patient. I'm still a bit foggy. Well, after back-burning all day, I gave you a call and then, when I started packing up to go home, Bill invited me for dinner. So, I took him up on his offer. I didn't know I was going to stay that late. It was just past two in the morning when I noticed the time and then left immediately."

"You rang me and told me you were leaving at six, and I was expecting you home at around eight. You shouldn't have stayed, especially after being away all these days!"

"Bill was my dad's captain in the fire brigade. I've known him since I was five years old. I couldn't say no."

"I don't care. You told me you were coming home, so you shouldn't have stayed! Or at least you should have called me. I was worried. Anyhow, why can't you stop volunteering?"

"For God's sake, Vic, can we talk about this some other time, please? I'm in pain here. You wonder why I go off for days at a time. Is there any wonder? All there is here is the memory of my dead wife and you treating our relationship like a business matter. I need a wash and another scotch, not the third degree and an argument."

He removed the melting ice from his face, half-expecting his face to come off with it. Then he stole a look at Victoria, following her curves beneath her nightdress, and noting those eyes that were so attentive to his moods. He had betrayed her again. But this betrayal had ended in death.

Why on Earth was Natasha chasing after him? He had always considered her too cool to act the part of the vengeful ex-lover. Men fell at her feet. If she had fallen in love with him, he was not sure what he had done to earn that love. He was an adulterer and although he was well paid, he was no millionaire. He was always surprised by love and resented the responsibilities of it.

Victoria's face had gone white and her mouth was hanging open.

"I am sorry if I worry about you too much."

"Look Vic, this car came out of nowhere and rear-ended me. It was a savage hit, and I was knocked out. The other driver had no chance. I felt like I was flying for a minute there. I guess it was all this rain, the storm, though I could see the road fine …"

"What do you mean, he had no chance? Did he die?"

"Yes, she died."

"She?"

"Yes, but that's all I know about the driver. The police will be getting in contact with me over the next few days for a further statement. The attending cop gave me his card."

He quickly pulled the card the senior constable had given him to show her.

"Okay, that's enough, Tom. Go on, give me the ice. I'm glad

you're home and safe. Even if you'd rather be somewhere else. The world is such a dangerous place at times. I do worry."

She moved again to kiss him but stopped herself. Instead, she went to make him another icepack.

6

He sat for a minute and thought of the years of volunteering, the lies, the women he'd slept with in different country towns.

After the death of his wife, Helen, he had felt alone with only her shadow for company. Eventually, he and his business partner, Victoria, had fallen in love but for Tom it was a love based on mutual understanding, propinquity, and shared needs and Tom always suspected Vic felt more sorrow than lust for him. Yes, he'd been unfaithful to her in a way he would not have allowed himself when Helen was alive. He hated himself for it but acknowledged that his affinity for the morals of the world had shifted since Helen's death.

He used to care but things had changed. In fact, he felt a part of himself separate when Helen died. It left a shadow behind, a shadow filled with a desire that could never be sated and a want for revenge upon the world that had taken her, needlessly, from him.

Now Natasha was dead too. Tom didn't feel cursed—he was the curse. Natasha was the first woman he had seduced for whom he had actually felt something other than lust. The others were a balm to his loneliness, he admitted that to himself, at least. And he had fled from Natasha as cruelly and curtly as he had because, for the first time, he had wanted to stay. He had not given her any notice, fearing that her arguments to stay would have been compelling.

Natasha was dead. What now? He could not cast Victoria out of his daughters' lives, not now that their grief had begun to diminish. Vic had filled her role of surrogate perfectly. It was not that he did not love her. It was just that she was not Helen. Or Natasha.

Tom took a sip of scotch and reasoned that this was real pain rather than the emotional pain and self-loathing he normally felt after returning home with the scent of another woman still on him. He sat facing the sunrise on the harbour, watching the light upon on the water.

Senior Constable Collins would be coming tomorrow, and questions would need to be answered. A chill went through him and he realised he had not yet allowed himself to grieve. Tom paused and glanced outside, and bright sunlight blocked his morning view of the harbour ferries' customary dance of synchronicity.

Then a thought hit him. What if the police had tracked Natasha's location back to the highway motel and discovered that both their cars had been parked there for most of the night? The room had been registered in Natasha's name, and Tom had been careful about his entrances and exits, which was pretty easy in a motel like that where transience was the source of their economy. Besides, in uniform, one volunteer looked much like another. There would be no CCTV footage of him, and they had never been seen in public together. In fact, their meetings had been limited to motel rooms where they had all the entertainment they wanted or needed in each other.

Tom followed Vic from the balcony to the office and then to the bedroom for a short nap. He tried to rein in his thoughts, but his mind continued to shout *j'accuse*. If the affair hadn't happened, Natasha would still be alive. It seemed he had a choice—petty desire or his partner and children? Lust or love? The truth was he wasn't ready to think about the truth.

7

Tom woke with a start a few hours later and immediately felt the pain pulsing through his body. It was still morning, but he felt he had slept through the rest of the day and the whole night. He abandoned all thought of his routine jog around to Shark Bay or working out in the garage gym.

Vic was still in the office working but the house was quiet, and he remembered that the girls were at school. He contemplated what his life would be like without them and recognised that because of his foolishness he could have lost them all—Vic, the house, and God forbid, the girls. That evening's dinner was not going to be ordinary. Tom also knew the bedtime kisses for the girls would be long-lasting and Vic's talk time even longer.

It had been several years after Helen's death since he and Vic had found each other in the same bed as if by accident. Victoria had joined Tom's business seven years earlier and when Helen died, she was basically the only woman he knew. She was always there to help him with the girls and after a few months, it seemed absurd for her to go home at all, so she started spending nights in the spare room.

Then, one afternoon, Tom found a note from Vic on his desk.

She had offered to resign, confessing that her feelings for Tom were clouding her business acumen and that she felt more like a nanny than a partner in a company. Lost in a haze of grief since Helen's death, Tom had been blind to the fact that Victoria had developed feelings for him.

Tom had resolved to stop his seasonal dalliances, aware that he was betraying Vic. But then he met Natasha. The thought of telling Vic was totally out of the question. Natasha was just a stranger who had accidentally crashed into his car on a stormy night, nothing else. His life had been so filled with grief he doubted it would matter anymore. Besides, he was now a minor celebrity, at least in the business world, because of what he had uncovered with ScamTell.

ScamTell had called Tom out of the blue one day nearly seven years ago, asking for a meeting. He had not heard of the company before, but a little bit of research revealed they were owned by two young men who had built their entire business around identifying scams and listing them on an advertisement-free website. All they asked in return for this worldwide service was a small donation from anyone who had managed to avoid a scam by first checking the ScamTell website. The 'Tell' part of their name was an insider's joke —they 'told on' the scammers.

Within a year of their launch, ScamTell was a million-dollar operation, simply through donations. The articles that Tom read about the rise of the company and the two chief executives, Michael Ho and Daniel Jackson, showed that they put their first million into the development of an anti-phishing app and software that tracked outgoing payments from any computer, funnelled the payment through a system of security checks and then approved or denied the payment based on a percentile risk factor.

After meeting Ho and Jackson, Tom was even more impressed. They were bright young men, neatly dressed in an Ivy League fashion and their employees were not carbon copies of themselves but instead were African, Arab, Chinese, and Indian men and women of various ages. Business awards littered the hallways, and plaques from grateful charities were displayed in the foyer.

The men chatted informally for a long time and revealed to

Tom their plans to expand the scope of their operations. They thought they had something to offer big business and government in terms of internet safety. Tom couldn't follow all their technical language, but the young men seemed confident that their next project would be of as much benefit to organisations worldwide as their first venture had been.

"We can't, of course, tell you more than that, Tom. I'm sure you understand," Ho said.

"Yes, I get it, but I just don't see what use I would be to you."

"We did our research just as I'm sure you did yours. We know you trained at Duntroon and served in the army and that you built your own business based on not only financial fraud but moral fraud."

"We know that you alerted East Bank that one of their investments was indirectly funding a firm that exploited coffee bean growers in PNG. And a year later, you uncovered an investment firm that was channelling funds from a Brazilian prostitution ring to a mining giant in the Kimberley," Jackson chimed in.

"None of that was ever in the press." Tom looked at them suspiciously.

"No, we delved into what happened when that bank pulled out of an investment with us. You see, we were doing a similar investigation, but we hadn't dug as deep as you did. Consequently, we made reparations to all those farmers."

"Yes, I had to go to Port Moresby to find out where funds were mysteriously being diverted. And the Brazilian thing was easy to spot but no one wanted to look," said Tom.

"Let's cut to the chase. We are about to make a huge proposal to the Australian government regarding our new product. We think it will revolutionise and make transparent much of how the government, banks, insurance companies, etc. use their money. Our money, that is. We want to show the mouth of the river, the river itself and all its tributaries," Jackson said.

Ho and Jackson claimed that Tom's credentials were top notch and that it had become known around the country that he had built his business on his ethical dealings with clients and had a reputation for uncovering frauds that were well hidden in the minutiae of contracts.

"For our proposal to even be considered, we have to make sure we are spotless, no funds going off to places we don't know about, no shadows over any of our accounts or dealings, nothing hidden. And every cent traced and accounted for. We know we have no skeletons in our closet but it's no good for us to tell people that, we need an independent and respected report, a moral audit, so to speak," said Jackson.

"Tom, we want you to investigate us. We'll pay you a one-off fee of one million up front. We want you to find any and all our faults. We need you to find all our faults," said Ho.

8

Tom faced the new day with dread, a slight hangover, and a very bruised body. He felt healed enough to do a ride on his stationary bike for thirty minutes, hit the speedball for twenty minutes and then warm down by skipping rope. He worked through the pain, telling himself that his muscles needed to work to unclench and that his body needed to loosen so his mind could. And anyway, he deserved pain.

He went outside to get the morning paper and waved to his neighbour, Charlie, as he drove off to work in his new black Mercedes with the top down. Tom looked back over his house. The sandstone was Helen's choice, but he had insisted on the jarrah verandah and the gabled roof, throwbacks to his childhood home. They were at odds with each other, but he didn't mind. He could see a pattern in it and thought it resembled his own psyche—slightly mismatched; slightly at war with itself.

Back in the kitchen, he made fresh percolated coffee and spread open the paper on the kitchen table. There, on the front cover of the *Sydney Morning Herald*, was Natasha staring up at him. The shock was enough to make him drop his coffee cup, the smash echoing through the kitchen. DEAD DRIVER LINKED TO SYDNEY

UNDERWORLD. "Natasha," he whispered quietly to himself. Then, he quickly rolled the newspaper back up, ran to hide it in his office desk and rushed back into the kitchen to clean up the spilt coffee and shattered cup before Vic and the kids came into the kitchen.

Later, safely tucked away in the privacy of his office, he retrieved the hidden newspaper.

A Chechen national, who died in a car accident on the intersection of New South Head Road and Bellevue Road early this morning, is believed to have links to the Chechen Mafia in Sydney. Natasha Mikula, 32, was killed in a head-on smash with a black four-wheel drive BMW during the early hours of Wednesday morning. Miss Mikula was the daughter of Vladimir Mikula, who is alleged to have links to the Chechen Mafia syndicate and is currently under investigation by homicide detectives for the murder of his estranged wife in Sydney in June 2001.
Although police have indicated that they do not suspect the circumstances of the crash involving Miss Mikula to be suspicious, they are investigating the cause of the accident and intend to interview the driver of the second vehicle involved, an SES volunteer returning home to the city from the Blue Mountains.

Tom had never asked Natasha what she was doing in the Blue Mountains. She had said her mother was dead and that she was living on her inheritance until she could return to America where her half-sister lived. That, he thought, explained the low-class hotel. But for now, she was happy to stay low. *The grave is the lowest place you can go*, Tom thought. Life had just got a lot more complicated.

"Tom, I'm making the girls breakfast. What do you feel like today?"

"Nothing for me, Vic. I'm fine. Hey, have you seen my Blackberry anywhere?"

"No. Why? Don't tell me you've lost it already? I just got it for you for Christmas."

"No, of course not. I'm sure it's here somewhere. I need to see what's on my schedule today because of the police."

"Sorry, how about another coffee while you look for it?"

"Fine, thanks."

The doorbell rang, making his stomach lurch in fear.

9

"Hello, Tom, and pleased to meet you, Vic. I'm Senior Constable Peter Collins and this is Constable Amanda Hawkins," he said after Tom introduced Vic.

"Pleased to meet you both," replied Vic, with a smile.

"How are those black eyes, Tom?" asked Collins.

"I'm just happy to be alive at the moment."

"You have a beautiful house, Vic," Tom heard Constable Hawkins saying as they walked down the hallway.

"So, you run your business from home? From appearances, it must be very successful?" Collins asked, as he looked around in awe.

"Yes, this is our seventh year in business and we're still on the rise," Tom said.

"Weren't you the man who uncovered the fraud at that internet company? What was it again? ScamTell? That was a whole lot of money there!"

"Yes, and that discovery was the making of my business."

"God, now I know why I remember your face. You've done some work for the local police department."

"Yes, and the state government."

Before sitting down, Collins took out a digital recorder, turned it on, and explained the process of Tom's responsibilities in recording his statement. Tom noted the device was basically antique. He wondered how the police kept up with all the high-tech crime out in the ether world of the net—the fraud, the laundering and the sixteen-year-old kids who were millionaires from cyber scams. Part of his work was to look into these worlds, and though he was no computer expert, he knew how to follow a trail. He had done that in Afghanistan as well but there he'd faced guns, not gamers.

"Okay, thank you. For the record, interview held at 357 Vaucluse Road, Vaucluse, with Tom Stiles. As you know, Tom, both Constable Hawkins and I are heading the investigation into Wednesday's accident, during the morning of March 1, 2006, at approximately four am," Collins read out loud from his black leather, pocket-sized diary after removing it from his shirt top pocket.

"I would request that you refrain from answering until after I have read out all the details. Now, the vehicle that you were driving, Tom, was a black in colour four-wheel drive, current year model BMW X5 with registration plates STIL02. You were stopped at traffic lights on the intersection of New South Head Road and Bellevue Road, when a 1979 model, dark green MG Convertible with private registration plates of MG 1979 rear-ended you. Why had you stopped?"

"Red lights, but I recall I must have been pretty tired because I actually got spooked out of a daydream by lightning, and recall pressing the brake paddle even harder while waiting for the lights to go green."

"Can you recall where you were coming from, Tom?"

"Yes, as I told you before, I'm a Blue Mountains SES volunteer and I was coming back from a backburning job, around the Faulconbridge area, up in the foot of the Blue Mountains."

"Who can verify this?"

"Bill Baxter is the Blue Mountains SES Area Commander. You could call him. After backburning all day, it was about six in the arvo when Bill invited me for dinner. So, I took up his offer and stayed. I didn't know I was going to stay that late. We spent the whole night talking about the old days, mostly about my dad."

He knew the police would call Bill, but he also knew Bill was old school and would lie for him. It was the code all the volunteers lived by—no one knows anything about another man's business, don't get involved between a man and wife, and what happens in town stays in town. Bill would have his back. If anything, the only risk was Bill lying too well. He just needed to text Bill with a cryptic *burn it all down* as soon as the police left.

"You see, officers," said Vic, "Tom's father was a firefighter and Bill Baxter was his captain in the New South Wales fire brigade, back when Tom was a little boy. Since Bill retired from the fire brigade, he's been running the SES in the Blue Mountains. It was Bill who encouraged Tom to take up volunteering. He does it each year and each year I keep hoping it's the final year."

"Your father is still a firefighter?" Collins asked.

"No, he passed away when I was seven years old. In fact, my whole family—mum, dad, and my brother—all died, in a house fire ironically, on my seventh birthday."

"I'm sorry to hear that," said Collins, as he glanced towards Constable Hawkins.

"Mr Stiles, have you recently misplaced a piece of electronic equipment?" asked Hawkins, blank-faced.

"Ah, no, I don't believe so. Why are you asking?"

At that moment, Constable Hawkins pulled out the large yellow evidence folder, opened it, and retrieved Tom's Blackberry mobile phone covered with a white powdery substance.

"I knew it!" Vic exclaimed.

"I've been looking for it everywhere … thank you, constable, but where did you find it?" He cringed as he asked.

"Our accident investigation unit came across it on the road as the deceased's vehicle was being towed. We ascertained that it may have been thrown out of your car."

Tom realised then that he had left it on the bedside table at the motel and Natasha had been simply chasing him to give it back.

10

Tom had not accepted ScamTell's offer of an up-front fee, saying it would compromise his investigations. He had told them he would take a week to think about it, shook hands and left the building. Companies didn't often ask for scrutiny; most had scrutiny cast upon them. But he could see the advantages. A clean bill of health, so to speak, with their AAA credit rating and reputation would make their tender more attractive.

And that was Tom's business. He did do some work on internet fraud and occasionally this work had coincided with police investigations, so he was asked to consult maybe once or twice a year. He had also done some work for the state government, streamlining the department's framework policy on how they assessed data. He had a fine eye for pattern recognition. Much of his working week was spent studying and tracking what happened with investments made by big businesses to check that the flow of money was going where it was meant to be going.

He didn't expect the ScamTell directors to reveal to him what their new product was, as they needed to protect their intellectual property, but they had made a good impression on him and all his further research revealed they were charitable employers with a highly developed social conscience. Both Ho and Jackson had campaigned in their youth against China's forced abortion policy and both were members of Amnesty International.

A week after their first meeting Tom had agreed to investigate ScamTell and made sure that both men knew he would need full disclosure and a complete history of their investments, personal and private. Within a day he had all their company files on his desk and he and his new business partner, Victoria Clements, went through every column and checked every deletion, contract clause, and deposit or withdrawal. In the first fortnight of investigating, they found no blemish, no hint of suspicion.

But then Tom discovered that in their third year of business, the deposit of an administration fee cropped up again and again and again. Victoria by then had also raised her eyebrows about monthly payments made to a company that was registered as a tapestry maker but whose premises were nothing more than a two-bedroom serviced apartment in Parramatta.

"So where are they making and storing these tapestries?" she asked.

In retrospect, Tom should have paid more attention to Helen's intuition that ScamTell were too good to be true. Early on in Tom's investigation, ScamTell made an unprecedented donation to the State Emergency and Rescue Services, a donation that was mentioned in parliament. Some coincidence, Helen had thought. Then again, he had wondered if Helen might have been just a touch *green-eyed* that he was locked away with Victoria for days on end and after all, ScamTell had a record of giving away a lot of money to a lot of different people and organisations.

One night Tom received a phone call from Victoria.

"I don't know what you are going to make of this ..." she said.

11

Tom scheduled a meeting with Ho and Jackson three days later in their new offices. He had not been in discussions with them in over four weeks and the information Vic had uncovered had led him to believe that the young executives were not what they claimed to be.

As he drove into the city, he flicked through the radio stations until he found Ella Fitzgerald singing *Mack the Knife*. Sydney glistened in the rain; a spectacular sight as he cruised over the Harbour Bridge and then eased into the left lane for the turn-off. He looked out across Luna Park where the endless crowds queued for the fun rides. Somehow the fun park's lights seemed much brighter than usual. Ella sweetly crooned about tugboats and cement bags and MacHeath being back in town.

He got out of the car, leaving the door open for the valet parking attendant and was on the thirty-third floor and in the foyer of ScamTell in no time at all. Although he'd never been there before, he was familiar with the new design of utilitarian buildings, held by one company then leased on to another when fortune, good or bad, struck.

Strutting slowly up to the PA's desk, Tom sanctimoniously

ignored the southern window's spectacular view of Luna Park and Sydney Harbour, showcasing the bridge marvellously, as he maintained eye contact with her all the way.

"Good morning, Mr Stiles …?" said the PA. She was just over five foot tall and was working 'the secretary in the office' fantasy for all she could—cleavage, silk stockings, high heels, and slightly askew glasses with deep red frames.

He nodded and his gaze strayed to the window. The view of the harbour seemed foreign to Tom from this vantage point. From where he stood, he could also see a spire of a church in the direction of where he lived but could not place it. Behind Tom a Japanese fighting fish circled in a large aquarium.

"Please go in. They're waiting for you."

Tom entered. Both men rose and shook hands with him, but Tom barely uttered a cold hello.

"Gentlemen, let's cut to the chase …"

Tom quickly detailed the irregularities that he and Victoria had uncovered—not only the payments to the tapestry business that didn't seem to exist, but the constant administration fees which the company charged donors every month. Tom could see no reason for this and estimated the company was earning six hundred thousand dollars a year from people who didn't realise they were paying such a small fee regularly. He then showed them a trail of money that went through three different bank accounts and was syphoned back into the fund that managed the superannuation for their staff. Tom reeled off figure after figure that was either inaccurate, incorrect, or imaginary.

"Tom, we know we have made some errors and certainly part of employing you was to find them—" Ho began.

Tom interrupted, "With respect Mr Ho, some of these are not errors. It's basic duplicity and theft. You have kept the credit card details for all your donors and made the transactions look like bank fees."

"No one has made a complaint," Jackson said.

"Actually, over a thousand people did complain and their money was refunded but you've preyed on people with the assumption that they would not notice the small debits and, amazed as I am by it, it has worked. The company that professes to protect against scams is scamming their own clients."

"Tom, can we see the whole report, please, before we respond?" Ho said.

"Of course. My partner will deliver it tomorrow."

"And you will, of course, keep this confidential for now. We will go through the report and make the reparations," said Ho.

"That is my charter. But I am obliged to report all my findings in due course to the appropriate authorities. You must understand, this is not negotiable. Any problems with this?"

"Can we ask you to wait a month on that? We've got our tender about to be reviewed and we hope—" said Jackson.

"Gentlemen, if this is the government tender you are talking about, no, I cannot wait. I have information that is in the national interest for me to reveal. I feel obliged to present this information to the tribunal that will look at your tender. My final question is, why did you ask me to investigate your company and then provide all the documentation that would allow me to discover this incriminating information?"

Ho and Jackson looked at each other.

"Tom, we hired you for a reason, but we cannot tell you all those reasons right now—" Jackson began.

"Wait, careful," Ho interrupted. "Tom, we appreciate your efforts and thank you for them. Believe me, we thank you for them. There's more here than meets even your eagle eye … please leave now before we say something we all might regret …"

12

After the police left, Tom ran to the bathroom and threw up. He could hear footsteps behind him, so he cleaned the sink and washed his face. He looked up into the bathroom mirror to see Vic in the doorway.

"Listen Tom, how about the four of us go out to Doyle's for dinner? We need to forget about all this. We could do with a night out."

"With these black eyes?" He smiled.

"They make you look tough. Come on, how about it? We have scarcely seen you this month," she said softly.

"Okay, where do you want to go?"

As he exited the bathroom, Tom's phone chimed, and he quickly scanned the incoming text. Silently he said, *thanks Bill, you'll never know how much I owe you.*

That evening, after school, they picked up the girls from Helen's parents and drove to Doyle's in Vic's car while his car was in the shop for repairs. They were seated at a table overlooking Watsons Bay. The water shimmered and cruise craft, ferries, and jet skiers crossed the water in what seemed like some beautifully choreographed aquatic dance. People waved and champagne corks popped on the beach. They feasted on prawn cocktails and lobster sashimi and drank everything the sommelier recommended with the meals.

One of the beautiful waitresses became enchanted with Vic's heart-shaped pearl necklace, Tom's last gift to her. She complimented Vic twice and then played with the girls on the balcony when she wasn't busy, giving them the seats with the best views and cutting up their fish and chips for them like a doting aunt. That left Vic and Tom to have almost the whole night to themselves and she whispered in his ear about the new lingerie shop she had found called *Elegantly Scant.*

The thought only made Tom think of Natasha. He wanted to imagine Vic in garters and long lace gloves but theirs had never been that sort of relationship. It had its eroticism certainly, but it lacked the tinge of danger that Tom desired.

Tom had a sense of uneasiness about the approaching day as he tried to sleep that night. Whenever that feeling arose, he knew his sleep would be short and troubled.

He woke a few hours later and contemplated getting up and doing a five-kilometre run but when he turned and saw Victoria sleeping, he felt swarmed by guilt and decided instead to pull in close next to her and close his eyes. Then he thought, *Chechen mafia. Fuck.*

13

Vic and the kids had gone to the beach the next morning by the time Tom groaned out of bed. If anything, the bruising seemed to have worsened, to have gone deeper into his body.

He checked his mobile for the morning's messages; a habit he hated in himself, making the damn phone his first priority ahead of kissing his kids or even using the bathroom. Normally there would be messages from overseas clients, new enquiries, or just his friends chiding him about the latest soccer results. But today, there was only one message from an unknown number.

Volunteer will meet Vlad. Come alone. Lobby of Four Seasons. two pm today.

The hair on the back of his neck prickled. *Perhaps it's a wrong number,* he thought, like the time someone named Justin had texted inviting him to his apartment for a 2:00 am booty call. But who would call him *volunteer*?

Tom knew it was the Chechens. He knew it in his blood.

He looked up an old friend to find out more about them. The following brief came back with his friend's name blanked out:

------------------------ *Senior Instructor, The Royal Military College, Duntroon.*

The Chechens are one of the Vainakh peoples. Society organised along feudal lines. Chechnya was devastated by the Mongol invasions of the 13th century and those of Tamerlane in the 14th. Vainakh bear the distinction of being one of the few peoples to successfully resist the Mongols, but this came at great cost to them, as their state was utterly destroyed. These events were key in the shaping of the Chechen nationhood and their martial-oriented and clan-based society.

He quickly wrote a note to Vic explaining he had a business meeting and went to get dressed. Then, in a moment of panic, he called Vic to make sure she was okay. He contemplated ringing up Collins and letting the police know everything. He had no business with the mafia. But he knew involving the police meant full disclosure. This would mean the end of his relationship.

He weighed this up against any danger he may be placing his family in. Vic, he decided, he could not control, but he might be able to control the external factors. And anyway, if Bill was as convincing with the police as he was with Vic, then Tom's story would hold, and Natasha's death would just be another Sydney road fatality. No use risking his relationship with Vic, not yet anyway. And what was one more lie to her?

But he acknowledged to himself that he was also curious. He could take care of himself; he was afraid of nothing. He simply wanted to know what they knew and what they wanted.

14

Tom detoured past the bridge in Vic's Audi. Thinking time. Michael Bublé was singing *Feeling Good* on the radio. They'd got his number; then again, that was easily done.

It's unlikely they want to meet me to discuss Natasha's last words, he deliberated. I*s Vlad motivated by money, family, revenge, or sex? He'll want two of those four.* He had no idea who he was meeting. After all, any immigrant with a bit of bravado, one good suit, and an accent could call themselves mafia. But in three minutes' time he would know who he was dealing with.

He pulled up to the valet parking area of the Four Seasons Hotel and headed swiftly to the lobby. He spotted two men sitting together in the empty lounge area of the lobby, each drinking coffee and reading a newspaper in Arabic. One man was bald, the other had short, orange hair.

He took a deep breath, slowed his pace, and headed towards them, noting the nearest exit, the six civilians and four staff in the rear. One security guard, unarmed. Twelve cars in the car park. *This is going to happen in public,* Tom thought, *they want to be seen with me. The Alekhine Defence, perhaps?* But Tom knew the counter moves.

"Excuse me, gentlemen, are you looking for a volunteer?"

"Ha! Vladimir, the Volunteer. He come!" the bald man said as he rose.

The man with his back to Tom turned around and put out his hand, which Tom shook. He then motioned to a chair, where Tom's back would be exposed to the window. Tom pulled a chair from the nearby table and sat on the opposite side. Vladimir smiled.

"So, you are Volunteer? Sit, Volunteer. Sit. I am Vladimir, this is my, how you say ... associate, Emin. I expect perhaps you to be intimidated by luxurious surroundings. Volunteers do not get paid, no? But you not look like that man ... no, maybe you will not be Volunteer? Maybe you fool Vlad, yes? I think so with two black eyes!"

The accent was deep, almost guttural, but there was a trace of at least two years of America. Maybe he had studied there or was even born there?

"No, I fool no one. I am a volunteer bush firefighter, you are correct. But my name is Tom Stiles."

"Tom Stiles, yes we know. Successful businessman, two children, adulterer. We will order coffee and—what is favourite of your daughters, Mr Stiles—*loukoumades*?"

Vlad folded and neatly placed the newspaper on the coffee table, not taking his eyes off Tom. He was testing Tom and defining the rules of their engagement. Tom knew it was time to get serious, or at least appear to get serious.

"You spent some time in the army, Mr Stiles?'

"You spent some time in America, Vlad?"

"Yes, I studied in America. But I went home straight after I graduated."

"And what was your degree in, family law?"

"No, Human Resource Management," Vlad said, apparently missing the insult.

The lobby was quiet. Emin turned slightly towards him, and with a brief and discreet flash of the inside of his jacket, revealed a silver pistol strapped to his chest. Tom was not surprised. It was the sort of move that might intimidate some delicatessen owner who they were standing over. Not him. He continued to act as if he were attending a tea party. He reached into his pocket and carefully pulled out a pen inscribed with his initials and laid it delicately on the table, as if it were a hand grenade.

Vlad seemed unnerved. He kept staring from the pen to Tom and then back to the pen. *If they wanted to kill me, they would have tried to already,* Tom thought. *They would not be sitting here ordering coffee.*

"So, what do you want from me, Vlad?" Tom asked.

"You fuck my Natasha, now my Natasha is dead, and you ask what I want from you?"

Vlad still kept one eye on the pen. *He can probably hear it ticking by now,* Tom thought, holding back a chuckle.

"I have slept with lots of women. I didn't mean any disrespect to their fathers. I like beautiful women. I didn't know who you were until now. Your loss is my loss too."

"You were going to marry her, hey?"

"No. As you seem to know. I was married. My first wife is dead. I have a partner now, though."

Vlad's sneer was replaced by a queer, yet almost genuine, smile.

"It will be okay, Volunteer. Do not be panicking, my friend. I see why my daughter like you. I like you too. Maybe not so much with two black eyes but you remind me of myself, maybe smaller, but dress good. But perhaps the colours black and blue suit you.

'My Natasha, she have good taste, like father, you know? Friend to Natasha will be friend to me. So, we are friends, no? My Natasha, I miss her, you know? But she listen too much to her bullshit fuckin' mother. Mother not let me see her for long time. Then when mother dead, my Natasha, she still not see me. Favour, okay? Friends will make favours for friends, no? Very soon, I call."

Which would mean what? Money? Information? An introduction? All Vlad had to bargain with was his knowledge of Tom's affair. Vlad had nothing to gain by revealing his affair to Vic. They were playing blackjack, but neither was the true dealer. If it were just a matter of blackmail, maybe he should just tell Vic himself. Tom said nothing.

Then the Chechens stood up and adjusted their suit jackets and ties. Tom also stood. "Call me if it suits you, Vlad. I have lots of friends, and I won't get lonely."

"Good, good, very good, my friend. I call you soon," Vlad replied softly.

Vlad looked around and he and Emin then made a swift exit through the lobby. Vlad was a small-time mafia wannabe from the look of his cheap suit, but Tom didn't know what, if any, connections Vlad had. It was best to play this thing out until the Chechen told him what favour he wanted.

Tom was not ready to tell Vic everything just yet. Not until his hand was forced. He could go to his old mate at Duntroon at any time or his police connections. *No use dramatising anything as yet*, he thought, *I need to protect my daughters' home. That's where Helen's memory lives; that house and those two girls.*

15

As Tom headed out the glass doors of the hotel, he thought back to the last time he had been there, just five weeks earlier for a meeting with potential clients. That time, as he was leaving, he had noticed security guards, side-by-side, leading the prime minister and a group of men, perhaps foreign dignitaries, into the hotel. And his old mate Hendo had been right there with them.

"Paul Henderson. What the bloody hell are you doing here?" Tom yelled with surprise.

"Tom, it's good, really good to see you. But I'm working. Can't you see I'm on the job, mate?"

"Well done, mate! Good to see you."

"Look, about Helen, mate. I'm sorry I wasn't there for you. How are the girls doing?"

"I got your card and flowers. She always liked your choice of flowers. The girls are fine, thanks, mate. Vic has been so invaluable to us all."

"Victoria, is she still with you guys? That's great."

"She's more than a business partner to me since Helen, mate."

"Tom, I can't talk now. I'm on the job. But listen, it's really strange I've bumped into you like this because I was planning to give you a call. I've got a proposition for you, mate. A chance to serve your country. The PM himself will want to meet you. I'll be in touch soon." Paul grinned and then he was gone, back in his place with the rest of the entourage, following some foreign dignitary towards the main function room.

That was the first time Tom had seen Paul Henderson since before Helen's death. Every chance he got, Hendo would always lament to Helen that he and Tom had both interviewed for the position of Director of Group Security at the bank they both worked for, and Tom beat him to the job but only stayed in the role for six months before taking twelve months leave for the army. Tom did return and take up where he left off at the bank before going solo a few years later.

Anyway, Hendo had landed on his feet back then. He had become the Chief Operating Officer of Bailey's, an investment firm known for taking over, and then selling on for a profit, companies on the brink of bankruptcy. But that had ended when Hendo resigned and turned whistle-blower, asserting that Bailey's was channelling funds to a terrorist group. This was never proven but Paul had been a *cause célèbre* for a few weeks.

Tom had suspected that in the wake of those events he'd been headhunted by the government. It must have been a steep upward trajectory for Hendo after that, as he appeared to be leading the security detail in the hotel.

Tom decided to take the long route home. He needed to think and to think he needed a quiet place, a sanctuary.

16

Tom drove away from the city but not in the direction of his home. He went over the day in his mind as he crossed over King Street, past the steampunks and Goths and university students queued up in front of *Clem's Chicken* and the Vietnamese pork roll stores. He felt there was a pulse to everything that he could not yet connect. A busker was singing Robert Johnson's *Crossroads* on the footpath to his left and opposite him sat a man holding up a cardboard sign that asked for loose change.

A car crash, the death of his lover. A Chechen Mafioso and the prime minister both wanted something from him and in both cases, he did not know what it was yet. And Hendo's mysterious statement about a call to serve his country. Tom would certainly do his duty; he was a patriot, he was loyal to flag and country, even though he had to admit republican leanings.

His father had been an army reservist. Tom's desire to serve his country was embedded within him from a very young age after seeing his father in uniform from family photos. Ten years as a reservist and another year at Duntroon, plus two overseas deployments duties, had sealed the duality for him—only the threat of war maintained peace. Only the threat of force encouraged negotiation and diplomacy.

He realised, crossing into Marrickville, that he was now in a position he had always tried to avoid ever since the fire that killed his entire family when he was a boy—he was a hostage to events he could not yet control or understand.

Tom reflected back on a training drill at Duntroon, where he was tasked with storming a small village, armed with rubber bullets and instinct. Some targets were dressed as civilians, and Tom had to look for a sign that distinguished them as he ran into the cluster of huts and a mocked-up marketplace. In his first two failed attempts he had died—shot by the insurgents. Then something clicked. He saw that each of the *angries* wore a red sash around their wrist, otherwise, they were identical to the friendlies. On the third attempt he had identified and killed each enemy combatant.

Returning to the present, he felt he was being played and to some extent it was his own doing. He had allowed his moral compass to tick over like a clock face.

17

THE CAFÉ DOORWAY WAS ARCHED. A HESSIAN MAT AT THE entrance read *fayito*. Tom entered. Three cab drivers looked up from their plates. Another man sat smoking in a corner. Steam rose from the display of rice, stuffed eggplant, lemon potatoes and racks of roasted meat. A man in an apron entered from the kitchen carrying a large skewer of blackened meat. He looked up at Tom and smiled.

"No strangers allowed in here, mister, but we can give you some takeaway if you know who is greater, Socrates or Zagorakis?"

"That is too simple a question," the smoking man said.

The other three men seemed to await Tom's answer.

"Vassilis Hatzipanagis," Tom answered. "He would have danced around them both. This you know, Giorgos. I will have my usual please and I will sit at my usual table."

Each of the men smiled and the man holding the skewer called out to the kitchen. A woman appeared.

"Tom, my son, where are the twins?" She embraced Tom and kissed him on both cheeks and on his forehead and made the sign of the cross over him.

"Today I have some thinking to do so, as always, I came here."

"So, you have not been thinking then for months? You are a

prodigal boy. Wait till I get coffee for you and then Giorgos will have stern words with you. Angelo and Sophia are like family to us, so you are family."

"As you say, Christina."

She kissed him again and returned to the kitchen, shouting out instructions in Greek.

"The girls will be with you in a minute."

Tom watched the usual reaction in the taverna when the girls were mentioned. The cab drivers tucked in their shirts and adjusted their ties. The smoker stubbed out his cigarette and sat up straighter in his chair.

Then the girls appeared, holding platters of charred meat, Greek salad, and fried potatoes. Each girl was raven-haired, green-eyed, and dressed in blue fustanellas. They didn't smile or return glances and it was only after they'd passed that the men allowed themselves to turn to look at them. They laid the food in front of Tom but didn't make eye contact.

The girls may have been beautiful, but they were silent and chaste. Nicknamed the *Maidens of Marrickville*, they had been promised to Greek husbands when they came of age and that 'age' would be decided by Christina, just as she had been the one to select their husbands. What made their beauty even more legendary, and the taverna itself a place of near mythology, was that all three girls were blind.

Tom ate in silence. The food was a balm to his soul, the food of his dead wife's country. Tom had a philosophical tendency which he mostly tried to suppress but he felt his mind unravelling over the events of the day. He had justified his repeated betrayal of Vic by telling himself it wouldn't hurt her if she didn't know. He never doubted that he loved her. But he did now acknowledge that it was an emotional betrayal to take a new lover each firefighting season. Each time he was being unfaithful to both women, and to himself in the end.

Since the death of his wife, he had been searching for something, anything, to assuage the loneliness he felt. He did not feel practiced in love the way Vic was; there was always some cold hard place in him, bullet-shaped, he imagined, that resisted obligation and the duty to love.

He chided his own pop psychology and reasoned that he just liked sex, he liked woman and women seemed to like him. Sex and love, peace and war, the government and the mafia, Vic, and the kids. What had he done?

18

Arriving home, he found that Angelo and Sophia had arrived. Angelo was yelling through the front door.

"Where my *engonia*? Where are my grandchildren?"

Helen's parents both greeted him with kisses and made the sign of the cross over him.

"Good afternoon, Tom. Oh, watch out for his bruises, woman!" Angelo yelled in Greek. Sophia pushed a large tray of moussaka at Tom while Angelo took out his wallet and produced two fifty-dollar notes, which he pushed into Tom's pocket.

"For you to offer to the sweet Virgin at church, Tom. You must do this for your children's health."

"Yes, Angelo," Tom said, though he knew the money was really to spend on the twins. Angelo would have donated an equal amount to the church already.

Hearing their grandfather's voice, the twins rushed down the stairs and into his open arms, screaming, "*Papou*! *Yiayia*!" The next few minutes were taken up with Angelo and Sophia bantering back and forth, in both Greek and broken English, about the planned shopping trip and how expensive the shops were.

Tom's in-laws both stood a little less than five feet tall, were quite pudgy in stature and despite their grey hair, they acted like a pair of children.

"Girls, we shop at Nose Bay?" Angelo asked the girls with a straight face.

"No *Papou*, we shop at *Rose* Bay!" the girls squealed.

"You really are a stupid man!" Sophia yelled. "I am sorry, Tom, he does this to me everywhere. Come here girls; get away from that stupid man! Come to *Yiayia*, girls, come here!"

Vic had organised it all and her timing was superb. She ushered everyone out of the house and into her car, instructing Tom to drive and Angelo and Sophia to follow closely behind in their car.

"Bell ran out the front door! Come back, Bell, come back!" yelled the girls.

Good, Tom thought, *hopefully she'll get run over by a car.* Bell was short for Tinker Bell, a stuck-up Persian Chinchilla that Tom regretted ever bringing home as a kitten. Back then, yes, she had been cute and cuddly and very adorable but over the years the girls and Vic had pampered her until she was spoilt, aloof and would often scratch or hiss when she wasn't getting her own way.

"It's okay, girls, Daddy will find Bell when we get back. You know she likes to get out at times to play and run around. It's okay, nothing bad will happen to darling Bell," soothed Vic.

They drove past clothing boutiques, specialist shops, and gourmet restaurants. Tom was still uncomfortable in Double Bay since Helen's death, but Vic adored it. She liked being amongst stylish people. *Like Helen,* Tom thought, who as a child of migrant parents was proud to expose her daughters to a more luxurious childhood than she'd had, working in the milk bar with her parents, studying commerce law while the milkshake maker whirred in the background.

Angelo and Sophia had been loving and successful in their way after arriving in a new country with nothing, but money had always been tight until Helen was in her twenties. They lived above the shop they owned, and things such as holidays or expensive shoes were not part of Helen's life growing up.

Vic was a private school girl who had spent her whole life surrounded by luxury cars and manicured gardens full of orchids and roses. She spent her holidays at the snowfields and attended dinner parties in mansions where she met eligible young men—the sons of bankers and lawyers. Betraying her for any reason he felt was no excuse, but oddly enough, he found her profligate past somewhat insulting to the memory of his wife.

He thought of his first meeting with Helen. He had just come out of Duntroon and had returned to work at the bank when he first saw her. She worked in the bank's legal department in the area of disputes and resolutions and although he had seen her around the building, they had never actually met. Then he oversaw the bank's quarterly audit, and Helen happened to be his lead contact for the review.

One morning, she had leant over his desk to place a file in front of him, and her hair had fallen across his shoulder. Her hair smelt like apples. She apologised professionally but she was blushing. He guessed she had never meant to get that close.

He made the three-day audit last two weeks, finding inconsistencies in everything he possibly could which he then needed to investigate, detailing petty cash claims against a thousand receipts, and finally clearing all the funding sources and expenditures with a manufactured attention to detail.

Two weeks gave him time to buy her two coffees, one of which they shared in a café. On the day he was leaving, perhaps simply out of relief that the audit was over, Helen asked him out for a celebratory drink. One and a half cocktails into the evening they were searching the city streets for a hotel and three hours later they were eating club sandwiches and drinking champagne in a king size bed overlooking Centennial Park.

As Tom negotiated the typical Saturday morning traffic, keeping an eye on Angelo in the rear-view mirror, he glanced over at Vic. The girls were unusually quiet, so he glanced in the rear vision mirror again.

"Hey, honey. Look, the girls are asleep."

"Fine."

"What's up with you? You'll be okay once we start shopping and you're busy, you'll see."

"Tom, I'm pregnant!"

19

Tom instinctively hit the brakes. Cars behind beeped their horns. Angelo beeped at the cars that beeped at Tom.

"Twelve weeks but I don't want to say anything to anyone until we have had a bit of time to get used to the idea, okay?"

"Fine, that's fine … we're pregnant!"

"Tom, who's Natasha?"

"What? You know who Natasha is, the police told us when they came over to take my statement, honey. She's the woman who crashed into me."

"I know you're keeping secrets. You talk in your sleep."

"I don't keep any secrets from you, Victoria. Look, if I do talk in my sleep, it's because of the accident, alright? Please …"

"Don't patronise me, Tom. I'm not stupid."

"What are you talking about?"

"You've been talking in your sleep ever since we started sharing a bed, and I've tolerated it for the sake of your daughters. And because I loved you, and I still love you. I realise that a part of you will never love me as much as you loved Helen. I've heard you say their names in your sleep night after night."

Tom felt like a wall inside him had collapsed. Vic had suspected he was having affairs for years because he had unwittingly told her. Guilt was not the first thing he felt but he knew that would come. His mind searched for excuses and alibis but instead he recalled the old cliché, the guilty man dares not sleep.

The list of names scrolled through his mind—names he must have uttered as he slept—Rebecca, Samantha, Christine, Suzanne, Natasha. He did not allow himself to dwell on thoughts of Victoria and all those nights she must have wondered about whom he was with and all those new negligees and sexual experiments she had greeted him with after each firefighting season. She had been fighting for him against women who were all the more alluring because they were not her.

He wondered how she had managed to keep herself together and why? Surely, he did not deserve her or the family he had betrayed. How did she fight against what must have been a revulsion to lie with him and to let him inside her the night after she knew he had been inside someone else? Why did she not say anything? Was she waiting for him to confess? For enough rope?

They arrived at the town centre's car park. Vic reapplied her make-up while Tom woke the twins.

Angelo pulled up next to them and chided Tom for his driving. "You need to learn how to stop, Tom!"

Vic gave Tom a weak smile.

Tom hated malls to begin with but now the levels seemed like layers of some fresh burning hell. The shoppers seemed neither real nor alive and the air tasted salty and reeked of food that had been cooked hours ago and was now sweating in a bain-marie.

All Tom could see was sickness and corruption. The pig carcasses hanging in the butcher's and the rows of chicken parts— thighs, legs, breast, wings, and necks—were all further emblems of death. Fish hanging on hooks. Fruit rotting beneath the shiny display piles and circled by tiny flies. Even the armless mannequins with their blank faces and glittering clothes suggested a circle of hell for the vain. His stomach turned and he almost threw up.

Vic walked well ahead of him with the girls, seemingly intent on easing her pain with retail therapy.

20

The drive back was a silent one, not a sound in the car except their breathing. Tom could feel the tension in Vic and the silence from the girls meant they could sense something was wrong.

As soon as Tom parked the car, in a flash Vic was out of the vehicle. She had the girls out of the back seat and had marched them upstairs before he was even in the front door.

Tom understood. A lot had suddenly changed between them and this was how Vic coped with stresses and strains in their relationship—she would throw all her energy into caring for the girls, keeping her distance from Tom, and giving them both time to process things. Vic made a fantastic mother; she was much more than Tom could ever have hoped for after Helen.

One evening, shortly after he and Vic had got together, she had opened up to him about her fear of doing the wrong thing by the twins. She'd told him how much she loved them already and how she desperately hoped that she and Tom were in it for the long haul because she couldn't imagine her life without him or the girls. As the years had ticked by, she had been incredibly patient and had never pushed Tom for more than he could commit to. Never had she mentioned a desire to have her own children; she just gave and gave to him and his daughters. He realised now that Vic's patience and tolerance had been much greater than he had ever given her credit for—she had known all these years about his summer affairs.

After bringing in the last of the shopping and locking up the car and garage, Tom heard his mobile chiming in the kitchen. Upon entering the house, he was startled to find Vic talking into his phone—she never answered his phone. His heart started racing.

"Can I ask who this woman is calling for you?" Vic said, passing the phone to him.

"Hello, oh, yes, of course … just a moment." He turned to Vic and whispered, "It's the office of the prime minister. I told you I was expecting this call."

"Oh," Vic said, chastened.

"Yes, this is Tom Stiles speaking."

"Please hold for the prime minister of Australia, Mr John Harlington," a professional female voice requested.

"Tom, I haven't got you at a bad time, I hope?"

Tom could barely believe that the voice from all those sound bites on the steps of Parliament was now addressing him.

"Hello, Prime Minister. No, not at all, sir."

"Good. Tom, we need your services. I'm hoping you can help us out?"

"Yes, if I can. How can I help?"

"I'm convening a conference on international fraud that will be held at Parliament House and then be moving on to Washington, which will bring together specialists from the USA, Europe, and the Asia–Pacific region. We believe your work on exposing the ScamTell fiasco would make you a valuable participant. I would like you at the conference. The conference is really a taskforce. We expect to formulate some worldwide best practice policies out of it. Outside the meeting room we need all participants to call it a conference as we don't want any public overreaction.

"Tom, before you decide, I can tell you that it will consist of twenty-five prominent and very influential leaders from within the internet fraud and financial security sector. It is a professional appointment, so you will be required to attend all panels, some in

Canberra and in the US, mostly. You will update me on all fraud-related national and international security issues. You understand? What do you think, Tom?"

"Sir, I'm not sure I'm qualified for this position."

"Well, you let me be the judge of that. This could be my last year in office and I would like to put a few things in place before I leave. There's a storm of crime coming, and we need to be prepared. Our country needs your services, Tom, so what do you say?"

"Yes, sir. It would be an honour and a privilege, Prime Minister."

"Good, good. I'll be sending a car to pick you up at six on Monday morning and I'll see you in Canberra before your meeting starts at nine sharp. Okay?"

"Do you need anything from me at the moment? And is there anything else you can tell me about what to expect?"

"Paul Henderson will send you more information about the conference and a dossier on the other invitees. So, please get to know the invitees and the conference topics. We have all your information. And I do mean all of it!

"Oh, and Tom, tell your partner and family that while you are away, they will be under the protection of government operatives. There's nothing to be alarmed about, just standard protocol for the families of government officials heading overseas on security assignments. You never know who is planning what, but I don't need to tell you that. You'll be known worldwide after the trip, so we must ensure that … well, let's just say, we need your mind free and focused on the job at hand."

"It will be, sir, thank you. See you on Monday, Prime Minister."

He couldn't keep the grin off his face. He had a prestigious assignment and the comfort of knowing his family was being protected.

"Vic, the prime minister of Australia has asked me to be on his fraud taskforce … sorry attend a fraud conference, starting this Monday. Can you believe it?"

"That's impressive. ScamTell really did a lot for your reputation. It's not another voluntary position, I hope?"

"No, and the prime minister of Australia rang me to personally invite me."

"I know, and I'm so proud of you. But listen Tom, I'm sorry about how I said what I said this morning. I've never had any proof, so I didn't accuse you of anything. But since the accident you've been mumbling 'Natasha, Natasha' every night. I have heard you say other names previously, so don't tell me it's just about the accident. What's going on? Tell me the truth and I will believe you."

21

"What truth, Vic, that I say women's names in my sleep? I don't know that. You tell me I do. Do I say men's names, your name? The girls?"

"Yes, you do."

"Then what is your overall assessment? You are accusing me of having an affair, a number of affairs. Is that what you believe, Victoria? And is it based on anything more than some mumbled, incoherent, half-dreaming words?"

"Tom, the other women's names, yes, I reasoned to myself they could be fantasy or just someone you worked with. I know you have a secret life, a secret past, and maybe they were ex-girlfriends, whoever ..."

"What secret past? My family died when I was young. I went to a boarding school then to Sydney Uni, the bank and then on to Duntroon before resigning at the bank to start my business. My wife died. End of story."

"Tom, you said, 'I love you, Natasha.' That's new. I've never heard you say that before."

"Concussed ramblings, empathy maybe—she is dead. She hit my car. Of course she was on my mind. The mind responds strangely to death, Vic, you know that. I know death better than most."

"We need to be honest. Did you have an affair? We are pregnant, we are having a baby; our first baby together and it's going to be a boy."

"Did you say a boy?"

Tom thought about the life he could give to his son and his life with Vic. "No, Vic, I have never cheated on you!"

The words did not stick in his throat. His face did not change. If anything, he willed his face to soften, to half-close the eyelids as if he were issuing a blessing rather than a lie upon his partner. He imagined he could feel the cold bullet inside him push into his heart a little deeper.

"Tom, I love you and I need you to take care of me and the children now more than ever." She put her head on his chest. *All the better to hear my heart breaking,* Tom thought.

"I am proud of you, Tom Stiles. The girls have an *Angelina Ballerina* DVD and a new tea set. We have at least an hour," she said, undoing the top two buttons of her blouse. She took his hand and led him upstairs.

They made love in the comfortable eroticism of man and woman. Neither needed to impress or tease or hold back or overextend. They had long ago mastered each other's bodies. They were each other's instruments. He found her earlobes and she moved on top of him, keeping one breast concealed beneath her lace bra and one pressed to his mouth. She asked for what she knew he wanted her to ask for and he the same, turning her over, running his tongue along her spine.

22

Afterwards, Tom went downstairs and took some steaks out of the fridge to thaw. The girls were excited, dancing around like the mouse ballerina on their DVD. He poured himself a Glenmorangie, adding some whisky stones from the freezer, and grabbed a cigarette. He rarely smoked, but in his office he still kept a carton of Lucky Strikes, a relic of his army days. His blood had been cooled by sex and the whisky was hot, making him feel dreamy. He dragged on his cigarette and his body rippled with aftershocks.

Whenever Tom smoked, it always reminded him of his brother, Terry.

They had grown up in Blaxland where the summers were filled with scorched days and heat that persisted deep into the night. To escape the heat one day when their mother had gone to sell raffle tickets for the SES, Tom and Terry caught the train to Central Station. Tom was paralysed with fear, but Terry stepped through the crowds as if the city thoroughfare were just another bush track.

They sat on the steps of town hall and watched the people pass. Tom thought the people looked busy and important but couldn't figure out what they did or how it could be more important than fighting fires. They walked through the big department stores, and

Tom wanted to buy perfume for his mother, though neither of them had enough money. He remembered thinking how beautiful his mother would look if she could have the lipsticks, hats, and scarves that the shop girls were wearing. They ate hamburgers near a fountain where a stone man was killing a minotaur.

After eating, Terry did something Tom had never seen him do before—he lit a cigarette.

Then they returned home. In truth, they had only been gone four hours, but it seemed as if they had been away for weeks. They had dirtied themselves a little on a bush track so they could say they had spent the whole day tracking brumbies, which was one of their favourite games. No one suspected anything, though Tom waited for what felt like years for their secret to be found out.

A part of him was still waiting for the judgement from his parents. In truth, he barely knew either of them and had only known them for seven short years; and from a child's perspective, but he felt his life journey had been undertaken beneath their eyes.

Somehow, he felt that his successes and his recent adulterous failures were known to them in whatever inexplicable way these things may be known. If he were honest with himself, he would admit that he had let their values down after the death of Helen. Helen had been a balm to the risk-taker in him. She was one of the reasons the business had gone from strength to strength. She gave him a security he had not known before—she gave him something to live for.

On his second short tour of duty in Afghanistan, he had been one of the four men who had volunteered to hunt down a double agent named Ajad Ajad who had gone off the grid in the Bande Pitaw nature reserve. Tom was the only one of them with any family ties. They were all orphans, but Tom was five months into his engagement with Helen.

Late into the third day of their search, Tom went off ahead to do some surveillance for the next day when he found a bedie. Tom remembered in the security briefing that Ajad smoked bedies but so did many of the people of the region. He followed a faint but fresh trail of sandal prints for about a kilometre until he came to a clearing where a fire was burning, and three hammocks were slung between trees. *Three versus one,* he thought. He reasoned he should just stay low and make it back to camp and inform the others. But he did the opposite.

He waited for the night to descend and for the three men to return to the campfire. They brought with them a wild boar they had shot and had portioned off the leg and hung the skinned carcass in a tree wrapped in spiked palm leaves. Tom waited. The carcass was bound to attract a big cat, which would make a perfect diversion.

When the search party arrived, they found a dead leopard, three dead men swinging in hammocks, and Tom gnawing at a bone. Three Kalashnikov rifles lay at his feet. Two days later, due to Helen's ultimatum that it was the military or her, he was on a plane home.

Vic came downstairs wearing an emerald green dress. Contrary to her earlier instructions to him, she suddenly couldn't wait to tell everyone she was pregnant and, after breaking the news to the girls, who were suitably unimpressed to know they were going to have a brother, proceeded to call as many friends and family as she could. Tom could hear the excited voices on the other end of the phone and expected that family would descend on them for a huge party the next day.

He took a second cigarette out to the front lawn with his whisky. The prime minister's call had buoyed Tom and perhaps diverted Vic's suspicions. For the time being at least. Tom reasoned to himself that one more lie to save his relationship was worth it. He had told her what she wanted to hear, and, after all, harmony was worth more than the pursuit of truth at this stage, for both of them.

Well, that's what he told himself but knew he needed to make some serious changes. For a start, he needed to stop all the bloody cheating, that's what he needed to do. And he had to stop the volunteering. Wrecking his family was not honouring his wife's memory.

The only problem now was the 'favour' Vlad would be wanting from him. He would have to find a way to deal with that, for his family's sake—for their future. Having compounded the betrayals with lies, he now felt more than ever that he had to keep it all concealed. Yes, he was honoured by the prime minister's call but any smirch on his clean image could see him disqualified from the taskforce and probably even ruin his business, given that it was founded on ethics.

Tom was turning to go back indoors when out of the corner of his eye he saw Bell lying on the grass near the letterbox. Assuming she was stalking some poor mouse or lizard and wanting to give the poor creature a chance to escape, he walked over to her. But strangely enough, she didn't move or acknowledge his presence whatsoever.

When Tom got closer, he found out why. Bell was dead. She had been shot in each eye.

23

Tom's five o'clock alarm rattled his head. Its one-two, left-right combination heightened the symptoms of his hangover from the previous night's family celebration.

Helen's parents had latched onto Vic as Helen's replacement, much as Tom had done. They treated her as if she had grown up in their household and shared the same customs. First, the feast with wine, then the dancing, some mandatory breaking of plates, then *ouzo* and reminiscing about the good times in Greece and the present-day troubles.

The only time Angelo ever got angry was when he talked about the Greek government. He was a silent communist who had taken what he could from free enterprise and like most men, lived with his own hypocrisy by justifying it as the need to take care of his family.

The bruises on Tom's face were beginning to fade so that he looked like he had gone one round instead of three with Mike Tyson. But his eyes were still a tell-tale red. It was not the ideal face to present to a forum where Tom knew that, within moments of meeting with these men and women, they would form first impressions that would impact on his relationships with them in the future. The leaders of countries, no matter on what side of politics, were often mind readers, adept at interpreting body language and most of all, good detectives.

He shaved and dressed in his best black Armani suit, leather shoes, and a dark blue Bell & Craven linen shirt. He looked instinctively for his watch and remembered the accident. As always, his black armband nipped him beneath his clothes.

The white government car pulled into the driveway and he heard a text notification chime on his mobile. He kissed Vic, wondering what he had revealed in his sleep last night. Several of the neighbours were out walking and watering their gardens and didn't conceal their curiosity as they watched him getting into the government car.

"Hi, Mr Stiles. Henry Lawson is my name, and I will be your driver here and in Canberra."

"Hello, Henry. Pleased to meet you."

"You too, sir, and thanks for not making the usual joke."

"Sorry Henry, what joke?"

"Henry Lawson. You know, the writer? People always tend to say something. Something neither witty nor accurate. It's as bad as if I had been named Don Bradman."

"Oh, I see. Forgive me, Henry, I am a bit slow-witted today. My in-laws came over for a party last night, they're Greek …"

"Ah, enough said. The Irish don't ever get drunk and the Greeks don't ever get full."

"Oh, they can drink too, Henry, they can drink."

"Understood."

Tom thought about the man he was about to meet—John Harlington PM. Tom had been hesitant in forming a personal opinion of him based on the choices he had made as prime minister. His backtracking on policies made in prior elections and his views on fighting the war on terror had not been popular with the Australian public and had left a bitter taste in most people's mouths.

However, Tom was enough of a realist to know that they were complex issues and that being in such a position might affect the decisions and judgements a person might make. After all, you can't keep everyone happy all the time. So, Tom was open-minded about the opportunity he had been offered, and if the PM of his country was asking for his best, that's what he would give.

"We're here, Tom. Royal Australian Air Force Challenger 604, the smaller of the prime minister's two aircraft. The other one's a Boeing 737."

"Well, thanks for the ride, Henry, and by the way, how long were you in the Gulf War?"

"How did you know that?"

"Your tattoo—three sabres crossing over a tank is a giveaway, mate."

"Second division. Part of the first wave of Operation Desert Storm. Yep, straight into the firestorm. I got this on my first leave of absence. Meant to be good luck."

"It was a straightforward bombing campaign with a huge mop up operation …" Tom said.

"Yes, but those oil fires appeared to go on longer than a lifetime. See you soon, Mr Stiles."

"Bye, Henry. Call me Tom, though."

"Thanks, sir, but I'm afraid I'm not allowed to—the hierarchy are sticklers for protocol. But hey, what was the party for last night?"

"Oh, let's just call it an early birthday party."

Holding onto his Blackberry phone, Tom headed along the red carpet towards the small plane standing nearby. The RAAF Challenger 604 looked like a corporate Learjet. He noticed the pilots in the cockpit, and the RAAF officer at the bottom of the mobile stairs stood at attention as Tom got closer. Tom reached over to shake his hand but the officer smartly saluted and quickly escorted him up the stairs. In no time Tom was seated and strapped in and the plane's engines roared to life.

"Good morning, Mr Stiles. This is Captain Edwin Taylor with Co-pilot Tim Shaw and Pilot Officer Ken Tucker," a voice came over the speakers and then proceeded to broadcast the flight details.

24

It was seven-fifteen when they pulled up at the steps of Parliament House where Paul Henderson was waiting.

"Hendo! This is all your doing, isn't it, mate?"

"Well, if he didn't want you, you wouldn't be here, so I can't take all the credit."

"So, are you the PM's advisor?"

"In some areas, yes."

"How on Earth did you get that gig?"

"Look, that will keep for another time, but now we need to get you through security and into the conference room. We've organised a breakfast with the PM for all twenty-five guests before the official commencement of the appointment of board members. Come on, just follow me."

Tom wondered what made Paul, and furthermore the prime minister, think he was qualified for a role on the taskforce. Hendo was ambitious, and Tom had always suspected that, after Tom beat him to the job at the bank, Hendo had been somewhat incredulous and resentful, perhaps even jealous. But here he was leading Tom, who he had recommended, to a meeting with the prime minister.

Paul introduced Tom to the Head of Federal Security, a man named Con, who handed him a security pass.

"I'll catch up with you later, after the board meeting's finished. Okay, mate?" said Paul.

"Oh, okay, Hendo, but to ease my nerves, can you do me one last favour? Can you get me seated next to the chairperson? That way I can keep out of harm's way and not look too stupid."

Paul's eyes widened. "Didn't you read the attachment we sent you, Tom?"

"When?"

"Last night, about eleven."

"What? No, we had guests."

"Jesus, Tom! Guests! You *are* the chairperson! You've already been appointed. Why do you think we went to all this trouble to get you down here? The others had to make their own way here."

Paul's mobile buzzed.

"Shit, I've got to go. Congratulations, I'll see you later."

25

Tom was whisked away by Con and led down a huge corridor. At the end were two large doors with security coded locks. Con entered a twelve-digit code and the doors opened revealing a modern, dark wooden boardroom table with twenty-five chairs placed around it. A smaller side table boasted an arrangement of fresh fruit, croissants, tea and coffee, juices, and bottled water.

"Please, help yourself, sir," Con said, escorting him towards the spread.

Tom poured some coffee but before he could sip it the remaining twenty-four board members arrived and swamped the breakfast table. There were a few tentative introductions which were interrupted by a sudden announcement, "Ladies and gentlemen, the prime minister of Australia, Mr John Harlington."

The PM entered the room and welcomed them all formally. Then he outlined the purpose of the special taskforce and how significant it would be leading up to the G20 meeting of finance ministers and central bank governors, to be held later in the year at Melbourne. The issues to be discussed included how civil society and public institutions can work together to fight internet crime, and how countries can work together in the fight against organised internet crime. Tom was unperturbed; this was his area of expertise.

"You have all been carefully selected to take part in my special taskforce because you are experts in your field, and you will advise my office of appropriate and fair recommendations that reflect the current climate of financial global security. Your efforts will be held in the highest esteem, and I'm really looking forward to seeing the results of these meetings.

"Now, apart from the press conference held here at the conclusion of today's meeting, I will not be present to influence your decisions in any way. So please help yourselves to some breakfast, mingle and get to know each other. I'll be here until nine o'clock, but then I'll leave you to your own devices.

"I want to thank you all very much for taking on this commitment. You have my deepest personal appreciation. I have every confidence that your recommendations will be of great value to the country. Without further ado, I would like to introduce to you all to Mr Tom Stiles, your chairperson."

26

Tom was not a bashful man, and he had chaired countless meetings before, albeit at a lower level. However, he could feel his cheeks flush. The board members turned to each other and murmured. The whole group seemed like over-excited school children and Tom wondered if he would need to play schoolteacher.

The prime minister appeared beside him and shook his hand. "Bruises seem to be healing well," he observed.

As Harlington talked, Tom was shocked to learn how much he knew about his life—the twins, Vic, Helen's death, his work accomplishments and how long he has been operating his business.

"Excuse me, Tom, I must take my leave. Once again, thank you for your commitment and I wish you the very best in your role as chairperson. I'm sure you're the right man to put out any little spot fires that occur during the meeting."

Harlington and his security entourage left the room, and the taskforce members scrambled for seats around the expansive boardroom table. *It's as if the music has stopped in a game of musical chairs,* Tom thought as he took the vacant chair at the head of the table. Feeling like he was diving into a pool of unknown depth, he took a deep breath and hoped for the best.

27

The prime minister burst through the doors of the meeting at three that afternoon with a media throng following close behind. Like the perfect host, Harlington introduced each and every one of the fraud conference members to the reporters and informed them of the task ahead.

The reporters simultaneously fired questions about how Tom obtained the role of chairperson, what his strategies were and what outcomes he anticipated. Answers seemed to come from Tom's mouth automatically, but his head was beginning to spin. Christ, when would it end?

When the frantic pack was finally escorted from the room, Tom grabbed his complimentary leather case diary and headed out the door.

Con appeared from nowhere. "Mr Harlington has requested a private meeting with you, Tom. I'll show you to his office."

After following Con along numerous corridors, Tom found himself in the PM's office. There was a magnificent portrait of the queen centred in the room and an array of family snaps on the large oak desk. Tom was surprised that there was no computer equipment in the room.

The PM emerged from a side door, flanked by three men.

"Tom, thank you for coming. This won't take long. I would like to introduce to you Federal Minister for Defence, Peter Constance, the Australian Security Investigation Organisation Director General, Jeremy Sutton and you already know Paul, Divisional Chief Black Ops."

"G'day Tom," said Paul as he shook his hand.

"Tom," Jeremy acknowledged along with a firm handshake and a nod.

Peter Constance, the Minister of Defence, approached Tom and offered his hand. "Tom, nice to meet you. I've been very impressed with what you have done with your small business over the past seven years. Though I guess small business is now an understatement?" He grinned.

The PM indicated for them all to sit as he lowered himself into the deep, green leather chair behind his desk. Then Constance turned to Tom. "I see you were in the Royal Australian Air Force Reserves for just over ten years. An explosives expert and an intelligence information specialist?"

Tom figured it was a rhetorical question but nodded anyway.

"Then one year round-the-clock at Duntroon. And during this period, you aced an SAS army regiment tactics course over at Campbell Barracks, Perth. What I want to know is how does the Director of Group Security of a bank end up an explosives and intelligence information specialist one weekend a month for ten years? And how did you manage to take a year off work to attend Duntroon?"

Okay, where was this going? They seemed interested in areas of his life completely unrelated to fraud identification. Tom was perplexed and wondered whether they would ask if knew a woman named Natasha Mikula.

"Well, I originally got into the RAAF Reserves to volunteer my time, one weekend a month, really as a firefighter. I was placed in explosives and counterintelligence simply because I was proficient in those areas during my training. The bank was very supportive regarding my involvement in the reserves right from the start. When

I requested a year off for Duntroon, national security reasons, they granted me leave. The only reason I resigned my commission was because I was getting married. So, I started a family and went into business for myself."

"Yes, we are aware of that, Tom," interjected Constance.

"I'm quite impressed with your record and will be honoured to be working with you," said Sutton.

But Constance placed the dossier back into his black briefcase with a peculiar look on his angular face. Did they know everything and just were not saying it, Tom wondered, or had the last few days made him jumpy?

28

"Now, let's get down to business," said the PM, leaning forward in his chair. "Paul is scheduled to meet with both the Directors of the FBI and CIA early next week in Washington, to discuss some recent developments in regard to the 'war on terror'. Tom, I'd like you to accompany Paul to have an opportunity to initiate talks with your US counterpart, Professor John Hull, who will be giving the keynote at the conference. I have organised for you to attend his quarterly committee meeting which will be held in the White House and chaired by the US Deputy Secretary of State, okay?"

"Ah, excuse me, sir, but wouldn't you need to send the director general for something of this magnitude?" Tom asked with a glance at Sutton.

"Yes, I have done that, Tom. But in this case, I would prefer a more informal and tactful approach and, with due respect to ASIO, they didn't spot the fraud at ScamTell. You have more experience in picking up anomalies that are less obvious. Someone of your background rather than a senior ASIO official may help to break down walls and I am hoping that more will be exposed, and that the interaction will be productive.

"That's critical for us right now—we need to be sure that our friends in the US clue us in to potential economic disasters as we don't want to be at the back of the pack. Paul will be flying out next Monday morning and I want you with him. Don't worry about the details, I'm sure Paul with bring you up to speed. Won't you, Paul?"

"What about the taskforce while I'm away?" Tom asked.

"Oh, don't worry about the taskforce. We will advise the members that your role as chairperson has certain additional responsibilities and that this short trip is one of them."

29

Tom's eyes were bloodshot from the lights and television cameras at the press conference and his head was throbbing after the meeting with the PM. Henry met him off the plane in Sydney and before he knew it Henry was pulling the car into his driveway.

He wasn't looking forward to telling Vic about his upcoming trip but decided it needed to be done sooner rather than later.

"America? Tom, were you planning on even discussing it with me? Or are you just telling me?" Vic screamed.

"Vic, just wait. I can explain." He felt like a teenager who had broken curfew.

"Don't you 'Vic' me, Tom. How are you going to explain to your daughters that you are leaving again? What do they even need you in the US for anyway?"

Tom couldn't answer Vic's last question. He had no idea why Harlington would need any soft ground information from Washington. No, there was something larger at play, not just with the Chechens but with the government as well.

Tom didn't doubt he had the experience and knowledge of international fraud laws to head the taskforce. Along with the other members he would develop recommendations that would inform a larger committee, the Australian government. It was no different from council meetings and advisory groups in regard to structure. But the trip to America was different. It sounded like reconnaissance, as if he was being tested for something larger.

Suddenly Tom's mobile started chiming and he said half-jokingly to Vic, "I need to answer this—it could be the prime minister!"

Tom calmed himself and answered.

"Congratulations, Volunteer," the voice said.

30

BEFORE HE COULD LEAVE FOR AMERICA, TOM HAD TO DEAL WITH the Chechens and be assured that his family was safe. On the phone he had agreed to one more meeting with Vlad, this time at the Australian Museum.

They had shot Bell as a threat; he trusted his instincts, so he needed to plan his strategy before meeting them. As his CO at Duntroon would say, "An idiot with a plan will outwit a genius without one."

Tom went to his gym in the garage and opened a large weights box. He lifted out the 20-kilogram dumbbells, revealing a stainless-steel lid with a keyhole. He unscrewed one dumbbell, took a small key from the hollow of the bar, and then inserted the key inside the stainless-steel cover and twisted left, then right, then left. The open box revealed an assortment of pistols, explosives, radios, military uniforms, and night-vision equipment. His heart started to beat rapidly.

Arriving well before the Chechens, Tom quickly reviewed the layout of the building and memorised the emergency exit diagrams in the stairwell. He then returned to his car where he sat until he saw the Chechens arrive. *Always let the dealer think they're winning*, he thought.

The Chechens seated themselves in full view of the entrance in the museum café, directly beneath a T-Rex skeleton.

Tom waited a few minutes then took a deep breath and strolled over to the café.

"Vladimir, Volunteer arrives," Emin said and straightened himself.

"Ah, my friend, Mister Big Shot now, huh? Come, sit, talk to me, my friend," said Vlad.

Beneath their cheap suit jackets were the distinct bulges of ill-concealed weapons.

"Mr Big Television Big Shot. I am in the business of making money, not like you with your government friends and your committees that sit and talk all day. If a pig is fat it is worth money. A girl is beautiful, she is worth money. A gun can kill, this is also worth money. Useful things make money, committees make useful things lose money. Why should a girl be beautiful and not make me money? Love? Of course I loved my daughter, but she was a beautiful girl, she is what you say … a premium girl. I am now asking for a premium price. Now you go to Washington. I need you to collect item from my cousin and bring it back to me. You do this for me, yes? My big-shot friend?"

"What is the item?"

"You collect something, that is all. No more!"

"What is the something, Vlad?"

"Something that makes me money. That pays for my daughter. You do this then you have paid premium price for my daughter." Vladimir's eyes flashed fire but he finished his coffee calmly.

"How big is the package and where can I find your cousin?"

"Package is small, my friend, small. You do not worry about this. My second cousin, he will find you. Nika Goesoff will find you, my friend. You do not worry."

"How small?"

"Small. Same as two hands together," Vlad said impatiently and pressed his palms together as if in prayer.

"How will your second cousin find me?"

"A man in debt should not ask so many questions. Save questions for your committees. He will call. He will call."

"Okay, and if I do this, you will leave me alone? No more favours?"

"Of course! Yes, of course! You hurt my feelings, my friend! We are friends, no?"

"I told you I did not need friends, Vlad. And what if I don't do it?"

Vlad shrugged. "It is sad but no matter. We all must make our decisions and live with consequences. This is the problem of free will. You make your choice, not God. But why would a man on the rise, a family man, a man of business want to ruin his career?"

Emin and Vlad got up and walked away. They did not look back at Tom, who aimed his index finger at the back of their heads, one after the other, and said, "Click, click."

31

Driving home, he kept Wagner on low volume and got stuck in the usual George Street blockade. He sensed Vlad had something else over him but could not figure out what. One affair was as bad as five. Victoria would not forgive him for one, let alone all the others, so what difference did it make if Vlad had done some snooping and found a trail of adulteries? Vlad was small-time anyway; probably a brothel owner importing European girls on fake passports or a stan-dover man who could out-muscle the weak and the easily intimidated.

Tom's business dealings were all fair and above board. Even the government saw that his mantra of ethics and profits was not a sham. So, what else? He had no skeletons in the family closet—indeed the closet was burnt and empty. He drove down through the tunnel toward home. Ultimately, if he did have to resign from the taskforce, so what?

I always want the cake and the eating of it, Tom thought. He was honoured to be asked to join the taskforce. It was a career step that might lead anywhere. But he was risking that by agreeing to deliver a parcel for a petty criminal to save his relationship. He was being honoured and extorted at the same time. And he had another child on the way.

The truth was he wanted it all, the job and the relationship, and the only way he could have both was to risk both. Tom parked his car in the garage and packed his unused equipment back in the weights box. He found Vic in the kitchen cooking *stifado*, kissed her, and passed off his meeting as another ordinary consultation with a potential customer.

When he went to ring Paul, he found a blue envelope with no return address on his desk. Tom opened the envelope and pulled out some photographs—one of Vic sitting at an outdoor café, the next of a man running towards Vic and the café, and a third of an old woman with her head in her hands standing where the café once had been, amid broken chairs and smashed glass. It looked like there had been an explosion. He had never seen the café or the old woman before, but he studied the second photograph more carefully. The man in the photograph was blurred but something about him was familiar.

32

Tom showed the photos to Vic.

"Who took these, Tom?"

"I have no idea who took them or why. Or why they have sent them to me now. Do you remember when this was? Do you remember the man?"

"It was about a month ago; you had not long left for the Blue Mountains. There was a flyer in the paper for the café and it looked lovely. It was all the way over in Chatswood, but I decided to make a day of it, do some shopping. That man, he came running up to me; it was a bit of a blur really. He said something was about to kick off at the café. I thought he meant one of the customers was making trouble. So, I left without finishing my latte—he was very insistent. Now I see why. I didn't even hear about it afterwards or give it a second thought."

Tom had no answers to the mystery of the photos. Why had the man saved Vic's life at the café? Or had Vic been the target of the explosion? Could it have simply been bad luck, he wondered?

He went back to his office and tried to distract himself with whisky and briefing notes for the trip ahead. It didn't work, so he played tea parties with his daughters and tried to explain to them where he was going and why. Sophia and Angela were more interested in feeding him imaginary cakes and biscuits and pouring him their invention of "grown up toffee"—a mixture of tea and coffee.

Tom put the girls to bed and kissed their foreheads. Vic joined him in the bedroom a little later, holding a glass of wine and looking very tense.

"Tom, something is going on isn't it? I just did some research, and it seems there was an accident at the café about an hour after I left. Who is that man? And why did he warn me away?"

Tom shook his head and rubbed his jaw. There was too much going on. He had no explanations. Someone out there, someone familiar, had saved Vic's life by encouraging her to leave the café before an accident? How could that seemingly familiar man have known about a random event? There was a gangster trying to extort him and the government were using him for something—he knew there was more to his assignment than the PM had said, he just didn't know what. He wanted there to be a connection, because otherwise there was too much to carry in his brain. He wanted an elegant solution.

33

Henry arrived at five past five, walked around into the red gleam of the car's taillights, and loaded Tom's bag into the boot. Tom looked up at the window where Vic was standing. He waved but she didn't wave back. She had a lot on her mind, they both did.

The city streets were just starting to fill but Henry sped through red lights and stop signs as if he had the grid of moving traffic memorised. Tom felt a sense of wonderment and calm watching Henry drive. Cars just seemed to disappear around him, and Tom sensed his youth might have been misspent at car rallies. It was certainly coming in handy now.

"V8s or formula one, Henry?" he asked.

"Both, and jeeps through landmines, military ambulances too. You just predict the danger and calculate risk versus skill."

"I'll remember that Henry, risk versus skill …"

"Challenger 604 again, Tom. I'll see you in DC," Henry said, pulling up next to the plane.

Tom was the first to board the plane but a moment after he was seated, Captain Taylor and Co-pilot Shaw marched onto the aircraft and stood at the front entrance in silence, at full attention.

As they saluted simultaneously, Paul strode casually onto the plane, flanked by Pilot Officer Tucker.

"Good to see you on board, mate," commented Paul as Tucker placed his luggage in an overhead compartment.

The two pilots stood at ease, then marched, in sequence, into the cockpit, closing the door behind them. Tucker then proceeded to close the hatch and serve coffee, first to Paul and then to Tom, as the engines vibrated within the cabin. Tom was asleep within one hour; not even the coffee could save him.

He woke as they touched down in Washington. Tom and Paul disembarked into a segregated section of Washington Dulles International Airport. An avalanche of salutes greeted them in the cold night air, and they were ushered to a black limousine looming in the distance, under floodlights and a line of red handheld night torches that were guiding the path from the plane.

The car took off at a terrific speed, and Paul laughed out loud. "I wouldn't bother strapping your seatbelt, Tom. At this speed, we'll be there in a few minutes!"

"Where's Henry? And where are we going at this speed?"

"To the house and yes, we are in one of the Presidential motorcade vehicles and this is their thing."

Paul had mentioned earlier that it would take around thirty minutes to drive from the airport to the White House—they did it in six.

"Tom, you stay in the car, mate," Paul instructed.

"Why, do I look that bad?"

He chuckled, "No, the driver is taking you over to the Hotel Willard. It's close to the White House on Pennsylvania Avenue. So you can rest up for the morning, okay?"

"But it's morning now, Paul."

"Look, just get back in, go to the hotel and unpack. I'll send for you at quarter to six. Okay?"

34

Before Tom could introduce himself, the concierge said, "Mr Stiles, you are on the fifth floor, in room 504. Please make your way to your suite, sir, and I will ensure that your luggage is looked after. And do not hesitate to let me know if you would like any refreshments."

Check-in done, Tom thought. Room 504 had a direct view of the White House. The suite comprised two bedrooms, each with an ensuite, a huge marble kitchen, and a lounge area with dark timber floorboards and a mixture of timber and leather furniture.

It was twenty past two. Sleep was out of the question. He opened the bar fridge and found a quart of Glenmorangie. He began to wonder if there was any part of his life that had not been scrutinised. Tom sat down and took a drink and then another. His life had been processed, surveyed, reported on, and probed into by God knows how many people and for God knows how many reasons. He looked up around the room and wondered where the cameras were hidden.

After quickly calculating Sydney time, he rang Vic and told her about the view and the room, how he wished she and the kids were there with him so the twins could have a Washington double bed and room service. Then he realised his conversation was no doubt being monitored and changed the subject. Vic asked if he was alone.

35

THE DOORBELL RANG AT PRECISELY QUARTER TO SIX.

"Good morning, sir. Special Agent Harrison. May I hold your briefcase for you?" said a six-foot-tall African-American man dressed in a black suit that was wired up for sight and sound from head to toe.

"No, thank you, and where is Henry?" Tom asked.

"Secret Service, sir," Harrison replied. "I am to escort you to the Roosevelt Room, sir."

Tom followed him to the elevator where Harrison inserted his elevator pass in a slot and punched in a code. The elevator went down for a long time without stopping at any floors and the indicator light stayed on the floor where Tom had been picked up. *We're deep underground,* Tom thought, *at least six levels under the car park.*

The elevator doors opened, and they stepped out into a corridor and stood on carpet emblazoned with an eagle holding in his dexter talon an olive branch and in his sinister a bundle of thirteen arrows. In his beak was a white scroll inscribed *E PLURIBUS UNUM sable.* Harrison indicated the way along the wide, well-lit corridor. Bright blue strips bordered the carpet where it met the light cream walls and framed pictures of the White House, past and present. One painting, Tom noticed, dated back to 1792.

They reached another set of elevator doors. Again, Harrison used his pass card. Neither of them had spoken since they left his room—the historic environment seemed to command silence. They turned right, following an arrow directing them to the West Wing. While the pictures lining the underground corridor walls had been quite modest and sedate, those lining the walls of this corridor were much statelier with shining, solid brass frames.

At the end of the corridor, Harrison stopped at what looked like double-strength glass doors with wood panel framing, and politely indicated for him to enter the room.

"This is the Roosevelt Meeting Room, sir," he announced. "I will leave you here, sir."

"Thank you, Harrison."

Paul was waiting for him, and other delegates were helping themselves to coffee. The meeting room boasted a grand wooden board table with seating for sixteen. An additional sixteen seats lined the walls on two sides of the room. Tom poured himself coffee while Paul briefed him.

"You will be sitting next to Professor John Hull. He's rumoured to be the next head of the CIA. The appointment will be announced next month," he whispered behind his hand.

"Good to know."

"Oh, yeah, don't forget to take your invitation for the White House State Dinner with you when you go. It's on the day before we leave Washington. It's next to your name tag on the table." With that, Paul disappeared through the crowd, escorted by a security detail.

Tom retrieved his briefcase and quietly headed towards the board table, noticing name tags displayed in front of each chair, each embossed with the presidential seal. Tom felt a sharp nudge in his hip. Off balance, he swung around to find a man in a blue pin-stripe suit, bending over to retrieve a pastry that had fallen from his plate. Reaching out to steady himself, his hand made contact with the man's bent back. Tom felt something solid shift beneath the man's suit and his mind went back to Duntroon.

36

Just as a person may be affected all their lives by the smell of shoe polish, a pipe, or a certain perfume, so Tom knew explosives. He knew the feel of them, the smell of them, even the taste of them.

Immediately, Tom went on full alert, subconsciously taking in the layout of the room and every person and where they were positioned.

At that moment, a dozen or so people entered the room, and a man took centre stage, asking everyone to stand. "Ladies and gentlemen, the US Deputy Secretary of State, Mr Robert Booth."

The crowd parted for Deputy Secretary Booth. He stood at the head of the table and welcomed all of them to the West Wing of the White House, wishing them a productive meeting and informing them they would be starting in ten minutes.

"You are in the fish room," the Deputy Secretary said, "but I'll leave it to you to find out the story behind the name."

Tom measured the imminent danger as Booth began to circle the room. He figured the man carrying the explosives would wait for his turn to shake the deputy secretary's hand and avoid prematurely attracting any attention to himself. Tom reasoned that given the freedom of the man's movements, his bomb was not designed to do maximum damage. It was most likely a one-to-one target. The assassin was a martyr, no doubt, but it seemed as if he had a bone to pick with America and not the other international delegates.

Tom pushed through the room, intentionally attracting the attention of security with his large strides and long arm movements. He reasoned he had at best two minutes to make a compelling case face-to-face with the deputy secretary. Risk versus skill. But as he moved, the man in the pinstripe moved as well. The man knew he knew. They were in a race. And the stakes were high.

Tom reached the deputy secretary first.

The deputy secretary put out his hand and began saying, "Welcome to the White House Mr Stiles, I'm sure—"

"Sir, there is a man here strapped with explosives," Tom interrupted, "Please leave now. Trust me, sir, please."

The deputy secretary looked Tom square in the eye, then gave a brief almost inappreciable nod and calmly said, "Mr Stiles, I will go and get that document for you now, please excuse me."

He turned and walked briskly, whispering a word in the ear of his nearest security detail as he left the room.

Tom turned and screamed as loud as he could, knowing he would create a path through the crowd just by the aggression in his voice. In addition, he knew he had to keep low as every security agent in the room would now have their guns trained on him. He moved fast and he hit the man in the pinstripe suit chest-high with a swinging arm. Tom pinned the man's arms and braced his head with interlinked fingers. He thought of Helen, Vic and his girls and he waited.

37

Tom counted down from fifteen. In those fifteen seconds he apologised to Vic, Sophia, and Angela, his parents, and to a God he did not believe in for all his sins. Once again, he had volunteered, but this time, he had volunteered his life. By reducing the impact, he might save the deputy secretary's life, but not his own.

It occurred to him briefly that his whole life had been an attempt at redemption. He wanted to redeem his parents from a long past tragedy he had no hope of controlling, influencing, or predicting and he wanted to redeem himself for the guilt of surviving when the rest of his family died. At this moment Tom recognised for the first time that his life had been lived to the tune of guilt.

A group of SSAs stormed the room, shouting, "CRASH, CRASH, CRASH!"

"People," one of them yelled, "this building is now in lockdown! No one leaves or enters the building."

Tom could barely breathe.

"He is lit up and loaded, agents. Get me up, handcuff me and check his back. He's wearing a vest, small distance, small calibre, enough to kill three maybe four people."

Tom was carefully raised to his feet at the same time as the suited man. Both had guns to their heads and aimed at their hearts and they were warned not to make any sudden movements. Two men in protective uniforms ran into the room and ran a scanner over the suited man, then over Tom. Tom still thought he was about to die.

"Lockdown, evacuate. Now. The Aussie is clean, building is Code Blue. Room is quarantined. Get everyone the fuck out now."

Then the man in the blue suit jerked his right hand towards his watch. Two gunshots went off and Tom felt the blood drain from his body. The room lit up and then went dark as if all the bulbs had fused simultaneously in the chandeliers.

38

Tom woke to find a security guard on either side of his bed. He wondered if he was in purgatory's waiting room. He wished his mother was near and then rebuked himself. A grown man wishing for his mother? *Pull yourself together, Tom, even if you are dead,* he told himself.

"Mr Stiles, good to see you awake," Harrison said.

Harrison is dead too, Tom thought.

"Sir, the president would like me to inform you that the Chechen emissary Lenik has been killed. The bomb detonated at about ten per cent; he killed himself and injured two others. Two agents. No civilians hurt."

"No other casualties?" Tom asked.

"No other casualties."

"The deputy secretary?"

"No other casualties."

"How did he get inside the White House with plastic explosives? And why?"

"We have examined the security footage and we know he was clean when he entered. But we also know he received three visits after his arrival in Washington from a man we think we can identify.

How he got the explosives is still a mystery, though. We are trying to answer that now sir."

"I thought I was dead, Harrison."

"I know that feeling, sir. Your body went into shutdown, adrenaline rush then full collapse. Scientists say that after an NDE the body can mimic death for three days."

"You can say it, Harrison, near-death experience, it's fine, mate!"

"Yes, sir."

"What's next?"

"Call your family; they must be worried. Then we will debrief you for the medal ceremony."

"Ceremony? And how long was I out?"

"You have only lost a day, sir. You got the all clear from the doctors to attend tomorrow's ceremony in your honour and your meeting that has been rescheduled before the state dinner."

Tom called Vic immediately from his bed. He explained he was fine. She kept asking him if he was sure. She told him, over and over, that she was proud of him and angry at him simultaneously. Harrison had updated her every three hours precisely, going without sleep to make sure she was well informed.

"You are too brave, Tom," Vic said. "And it won't do any of us any good."

Making his way back to his room to clean and rest up, Harrison picked up some morning newspapers and put them on Tom's lap.

"I'll have room service send up some breakfast. Happy reading."

AUSSIE HERO THWARTS WHITE HOUSE TERROR.

Gobsmacked, Tom stared at the headline of *The New York Times* and at his own face printed below it.

39

After the pompous ceremony headed by a very appreciative deputy secretary, Tom made his way back to the Roosevelt Room for his rescheduled meeting and was astonished to see everyone else in the room was already seated with all bar his own seat at the table occupied and even the seats lining both walls all taken. He took his seat next to the very thankful deputy secretary. As he sat, the delegates all stood and applauded.

The deputy secretary took charge. "Ladies and gentlemen and distinguished board members. I thank you all for your patience as we allowed Mr Stiles to recuperate. By your applause I see that you understand the magnitude of what Mr Stiles did. I think it is now best to move on as the president has asked me to do.

"My first order is to take this opportunity to welcome you all back to the Roosevelt Room here at the White House. A special welcome also goes to our two distinguished guests, Professor John Hull and Mr Tom Stiles, who the world now knows and someone to whom we are all very grateful.

"I would like to thank you all for attending this very significant special meeting. As Chairman, I would like to ask for quick, around-the-table introductions and encourage all participants to engage in discussion so that all viewpoints are heard.

"Mr Stiles has been sent here by Prime Minister John Harlington to gather a snapshot, so to speak, of our US economy and its state of affairs, and furthermore, to strengthen the US and Australian economic relationship in the lead-up to the G20 Summit in Australia in November. I also believe Mr Stiles has prepared a short introductory speech to begin our meeting this morning, and I invite Professor Hull and all our special guests to table anything you have prepared once Mr Stiles concludes. So please welcome Mr Stiles."

Tom rose and went to the main lectern. "Thank you, Mr Deputy Secretary. I would like to start off this meeting with a quote by the French philosopher, Professor Alain Badiou—'The ethic of truth is the complete opposite of an "ethics of communication". It is an ethic of the Real ... The ethic of truth is absolutely opposed to opinion, and to ethics in general.'

"Professor Badiou puts it clearly that, irrespective of the demands and pressures upon it, business is bound to be ethical for two reasons—one, because whatever the business does affects its stakeholders, and two, because every juncture of action has trajectories of ethical as well as unethical paths, wherein the existence of the business is justified by ethical alternatives it responsibly chooses.

"I don't need to remind you all of the numerous corporate scandals and mammoth collapses between 2001 and 2004 that affected large corporations in the US like Enron, Arthur Anderson, WorldCom and Tyco, not to mention what has also happened globally. I believe these multinationals have their core business ethics to blame for their demise. Our best and our brightest were running these corporations. A major foreign power using terrorism didn't do this to all of us, *we* did this to *ourselves*, distinguished guests.

"Professor Badiou asks for paradigm shift with regard to ethics. The goal of epistemology is to add awareness to knowledge. Ethics, ladies and gentlemen, need to be entrenched and rooted deep down in our beliefs by, I believe, a modern pedagogy approach to corporate ethics within our business schools and universities. This is why deliberation for a more proactive approach needs to be taken with governance by strengthening legislation and government controls.

"This must be a starting point of our discussion here today because our mutual core beliefs of capitalism affect our politics and our way of democracy. Taking a tokenistic, academic approach or playing on semantics at this meeting now is not good enough, ladies and gentlemen. It's time to talk about real, ethical approaches in the way we do business, or we will fail our politicians, our governments and, ultimately, our constituents, friends and families."

Tom finished with a tight fist, sat back down, and took a drink of water. The room was quiet for a while. The Deputy Secretary turned towards Tom and stared at him, clearly not impressed. And when the meeting finally concluded, with some regret, he overheard one delegate passing behind him muttered, "I never did like the French …"

Maybe I should stick to saving lives, Tom thought.

40

On his way out, Tom checked his mobile for messages. There was a missed call from an unknown number. Vlad's second cousin, he guessed.

But Tom heard a female voice with a clear mid-western American accent. She wanted him to meet her that evening at seven in the Round Robin Bar. The State Dinner was at eight, with pre-dinner drinks at seven-thirty, so he figured he had time to meet her briefly.

At five to seven Tom was dressed in a tuxedo and in the Round Robin. He took a seat on one of the only two bar stools left, closest to the street exits and where the bar seemed least crowded.

His eyes roved over the signed photos of Jimmy Connors and John McEnroe on the walls. Behind the bar was a twelve-foot-long tennis racquet and above the bar the light bulbs glowed bright green like tennis balls. Sting played on the jukebox and the waitresses wore short white skirts. No one in the crowd was taking the joint or themselves too seriously; it was as chilled as the Glenmorangie that Tom had just ordered.

Tom scanned the crowd. Rich students, congressmen's wives,

one or two who waved at him, a couple of B-grade celebrities surrounded by flunkies and at least two businessmen high on cocaine. Tom grinned to himself. The waitress brought his drink and asked for no payment, though Tom decided he would tip her a redback as he was leaving. She turned and smiled and called him a sweetheart after yelling out, "Aussie currency is my favourite!"

Then Tom saw a ghost.

Natasha walked towards him through the crowd in a dark blue, strapless cocktail dress split up to her thigh. He was spellbound, afraid, unbelieving, ecstatic. Her long, blonde hair bounced on her shoulders with every stride. Was she back from the dead? Or was there something wrong with his brain? In the hours it seemed to take for her to cross over to him, Tom questioned his own sanity, the contents of his drink and the hallucinatory effects of the tennis ball lights.

"I am Anna Goesoff, Mr Stiles." She smiled, her eyes flicking over him.

"I watched you from a distance, Anna, and you didn't look around or hesitate. How did you know it was me you were meeting?"

"I noticed I caught your attention. Besides, your face is all over the media."

"So, you are Natasha's half-sister, I didn't realise you were so identical. It's remarkable. Except your beauty spot is on the opposite cheek."

A waitress arrived with another Glenmorangie for Tom and a Martini, no olive, for Anna. *She even smells like Natasha,* Tom thought.

"I cannot make small talk now. I am here only to make contact with you, that is all. I will meet you here tomorrow, at the same time, and deliver the package to you. Do you understand?"

Tom nodded. Anna tilted her neck slightly and downed her drink, placing her near-empty glass on the bar. As she stood, the slit in her dress parted, revealing a garter belt and red suspenders. She caught Tom's eye, opened the slit a little further, put her finger in her mouth and bit down hard. Then she closed the slit and walked off. Tom gulped his drink and motioned no when offered another. *Tomorrow will take an eternity to arrive,* he thought. As she left the bar Anna turned once more and smiled.

41

Tom showed security his invitation and was waved on through the gates. Other patrons arrived by chauffeured limousine. Tom liked that he alone was on foot.

As he entered the White House an announcer said, "Mr Tom Stiles, honorary patriot and national hero!"

Cameras clicked, microphones appeared, and a fusillade of questions were shot at him until agents escorted Tom through the press to the South Lawn, where Paul sat amongst esteemed presidential guests at one of ten long tables, sipping a highball. The garden was set up with linen-fringed tables and bouquets of freesias, the favourite flower of the president's wife, Tom remembered. Small, fluted candles lit the pathways and a quartet of violinists, all female, all wearing long, flowing black gowns, were playing Vivaldi. Paul greeted Tom's escort in full military fashion, and they retreated.

"So, Tom, have you settled into being a national hero?"

"Wish Vic saw it that way. She's not so impressed with my antics."

"Forget that for now. You're here for a higher purpose and I don't mean just the fraud talks."

"Spit it out, mate." Tom had suspected all along that the conference was a front for something else. He now waited for Paul to play the full hand.

"Think about it, Tom," Paul began, "you built a business on ethics. Ethics became your trademark. You rose to success on that trademark and people went looking for something in your past. What they found was military training and explosives expertise—in short, a potential killer. With your business and your family, even your bravery at a local level as a volunteer firefighter, you have built a cover for yourself without knowing it."

"A cover for what?"

"Elite A level Agency. Tom, you have the core material to be a spook. I've been ordered by the PM to offer you a place on my team, SFA level—wet status, effective as soon as we return to Aussie soil. The Deputy Secretary was so impressed by your save the other day, he called the PM immediately and the decision was made. They went through your past and saw you'd been commended for your tours of duty in Afghanistan. Truth is, the PM, the defence minister and the director have been considering you for a while now, ever since ScamTell."

"Paul, be serious, I'm a family man. A businessman. I chose not to take on that life years ago. Now I hunt people in a different way—no guns or bombs, just spreadsheets and a little bit of computer hacking. If anything, after this trip I'm better known now than before. All America and half the world have seen my face. Aren't spooks meant to be underground, anonymous?"

"Sometimes it's more effective to be invited to a party than to gatecrash it."

"SFA level—wet status ... what's that?"

"Elite ASIO agents who work with our US counterparts on covert missions are authorised wet team, meaning green light assassins. Permission to kill. The PM would like you to take on a covert dual operation in and out of Australia and the US, relating to unusual financial activity, targeting diplomats and high-ranking attachés. Your cover will be real—you're a fraud expert working on the new taskforce.

"This is part of a new initiative, Black Ops: Zulu. Australia is now working closer than ever with our US allies. The PM has just committed to this new covert initiative with the US to help fight the war on terror. It's the new way, Tom. At BOZ we do what ASIO doesn't have the balls to do. That's why you're here and not talking to the head of ASIO. You'll be putting out fires, Tom. It's what you do best."

42

"Paul. I have a family and I run a business. I'm not a spy, and I'm not a killer."

"You're the one who made the save, Tom."

"Look, I don't give a damn. That was just doing what a man had to do. I'm only here because the PM requested it, okay?"

"Not every man risks his life, Tom. Not every family man or businessman has the instinct and fearlessness to act. The PM has asked for you, Tom, to volunteer. Think about it mate, you're a world figure now. You can enter any country on the briefest of security checks and the flimsiest of pretexts. You just disarmed a terrorist working only on instinct!"

"I just got lucky. The right place at the right time. That's all."

"No, Tom. That's not all. You're now a challenge. Half the corrupt organisations in the world, whether they're fronts for terror, the drug trade, or the civilian upheaval of a government, will now want to buy you. Who better to front evil than the man who is stainless? Think about it, mate, if you want to be seen as being straight in the eyes of the law, ask for an ethical man to investigate you."

Tom snatched another glass of champagne from one of the

many passing drink waiters. Paul stood, smiled, and strode away. Tom watched as he began an intense discussion with a man wearing twelve medals on his uniform. *More confetti than a wedding,* Tom thought.

43

THE DINNER BELL CHIMED. BEFORE THE PRESIDENT CAME OUT, A beautiful black woman wearing a silver sequinned dress sang an acappella rendition of the national anthem. Everyone stood and put their hands on their hearts.

Then, amidst blaring trumpets, the president arrived with his wife and two young daughters, both just a little older than Tom's. He made a short welcome speech and people resumed their seats as waiters brought the first course of oysters. To Tom's amusement they were Sydney rock oysters, declared in the menu as the best oysters in the world. Paul lifted one in the air and toasted Tom silently, and they both smiled and slugged them back.

Between courses Tom made his way over to Paul's table. *What table here isn't a power table?* Tom thought, looking around at congressmen, senators, and their glamorous wives who were themselves probably all Columbia or Yale graduates and who all no doubt headed charitable causes, not because they were saints, but because that in itself was campaigning for their husbands. Then there were the female senators, each displaying acute wit and perfect grooming, and a millionaire beau who looked like he'd just stepped out of a sanatorium.

Paul introduced Tom to the men and women around the table—Wall Street merchants riding high on bonds, the dean of Yale, a movie star who Tom recognised from a trilogy of bad action movies, and the GM of the Washington Redskins. The businessmen wanted to talk sport or Hollywood and the Hollywood star wanted to talk about human rights in China. Tom listened to them intently.

"If we get this kid we're after from Penn State in the mid-season draft, we'll make the playoffs," the GM said. "Put money on it."

"Can't I put money into getting you the kid, then put money on it?" a smiling businessman asked.

"Sure can. We can talk later, Jerry."

"So, tell me, gentlemen, is investing in football less risky than investing in a Hollywood movie?" the actor asked.

"It is all risk management, balance of probabilities, rat cunning," the businessman replied.

"Rat cunning had all the rats recently fleeing a sinking ship, if I remember correctly," the dean said.

"On a long enough timeline, everyone's survival rate drops to zero. Now if your timeline starts on borrowed time, every day you stay alive is a miracle. Miracles are not probable."

"So, what runs the market now?" the actor asked.

"An absolute faith in miracles."

44

EVERYONE AT THE TABLE SMILED BUT NONE OF THEM LOOKED comfortable.

Two college professors began discussing the problem with China's boom. "No one can compete with China on price. China sells vast quantities of goods to the rest of the world, without the rest of the world having any chance of selling similar quantities to China! Like Japan used to say, we don't buy, we sell."

"And no one sells to those who sell to them. It's open slather and it creates a structural imbalance."

"So where does this imbalance lead?"

"Well, we've seen the iceberg and now it may really tip ... look at Europe. Democracy as a level playing field was always a lie. You only get rich by making someone else poor. Money makes money."

"So, the end of democracy?"

"As an ideal, yes. What does it do for the unemployed? The disenfranchised? Isn't India the biggest democracy in the world, with also the biggest percentile difference between the poor and the middle class, the most polluted environment, the most impoverished people?"

"Poverty leads to anger, anger leads to violence, violence leads to change?"

"Endgame?"

Tom turned to the Redskins GM who had hardly said a word and wore a bored expression. "I guess your work means you rarely get time to focus on economies and such?"

"On the contrary, all sport is focused on economy, we're all trying to minimise our losses and maximise our gains. But one thing we have learnt that others don't seem to have learnt is that you don't need to lose anything."

"I don't know much about the NFL," Tom said. "I follow soccer, but I do know that all companies have to give something, lose something, even if we're talking wages."

"Yes, of course, but wages are not a loss if you're getting back more than you paid for. We had all these guys coming out with Masters of Business from Yale and Harvard, and master statisticians and the best fitness people, and giving us all the so-called relevant or revolutionary data and business models and we were coming last."

"So, what changed? You just won the title, yes?"

"The last two actually. We reduced everything to one simple premise—what is the simplest method that works and how much does simplicity cost? We just got guys in every department who did one job well, not brilliantly, just well enough. We did the same on the field, and we coordinated it all so every person just did their job, not more or less. They were cogs, sure, but the clock kept ticking.

"We just defined what we wanted—to win—and found the simplest way to win and got everyone to buy in. We were limited in what we could do by the draft, salary caps etc., but as the poet once said, 'Limitation makes for power. The strength of the genie comes from him being confined in a bottle.' We did what we could with what we had, we saved money, we won. The world is too complicated for its own good."

45

Tom could see the trouble ahead looming for the global economy. In hindsight, it had begun when the US ignored a fair balance of trade in the 1970s and just printed more money to cover its imports, abandoning the gold standard. But then the Euro rats became cunning and wanted payment in gold rather than American dollars. The butterfly wings started flapping back. Then Vesuvius rained down on the world banks and, in turn, governments.

In his role on the International Fraud Taskforce, Tom was looking for the next butterfly and he had to net it, preserve it, pin it, and present it to the prime minister. He was sure he could find it, the next major fraud, hidden in the wings of the butterfly.

And perhaps the butterfly would represent the simplest things—in a world where we can talk to someone face to face whilst being a thousand miles away, where all our movements can be tracked, all our calls heard, all our emails re-read and all these things are protected by firewalls and security networks, how can you reduce your life to simplicity? How can you disappear?

Beef Wellington with hassleback potatoes and collard greens—apparently the president's favourite—arrived and conversation slowed as everyone ate. The entertainment was the U2 concert beamed in live from Central Park on a big screen. Bono was singing *I Still Haven't Found What I'm Looking For*.

46

He needed to escape the dinner. The synapses in his brain were starting to hum with energy, energy that was only partly due to the memory of Anna's dress.

Back in his hotel room, he changed into boxer shorts and a Bonds singlet, took a Budweiser from the mini-bar, and sat down at the table to put his thoughts on paper. The ideas were like a cloud formation that was starting to resemble a figure of some kind, neither definite nor concrete, that would be, of course, defined by the eye of the viewer. Snippets of conversations Tom had overheard at the State Dinner replayed in his mind and intersected and merged with these ideas.

Tom worked on his notes, trying to fashion a whole out of his fragmented thoughts, trying to think globally and provincially at the same time. He balanced, calculated, and forecasted, searching for the next butterfly.

His phone chimed with a text from Paul, a demand that he meet him for breakfast at seven forty-five the next morning. His mind drifted to Paul's offer. What would it mean to his life? The lives of his family? How could a father of soon to be three take on a role as an international assassin? It was a ridiculous proposition and much too risky. How could those two lives coexist?

But he recognised a tug in himself, not to the glamour and certainly not to killing. His sense of loyalty had been triggered, his pride had been tapped, and in the end, he had to admit that uncovering internet and money fraud was boring—there was no adrenaline in it. For God's sake, the President of the United States and the Prime Minister of Australia had called on him, who was he to say no? In addition, his recent dealings with Vlad and his introduction to the world of small-time crime had awoken something in him. He had felt the urge to risk himself again unlike any time since Duntroon.

There was something else. He guessed it was called vanity. Here he was in the company of the world's elite and he felt at home, at ease, even. He realised this was the world he'd always yearned for. This was the elusive answer he had been seeking his whole life. Or at least, in his life post-Helen.

He had always acknowledged to himself, with nothing other than pride, that he had quit all military deployments and stayed the course of his financial training to make sure he was first a good husband to Helen and then a good provider for his children. He had put aside the riskier options of staying on in the military, becoming a firefighter like his father or even pursuing a career in the stock market to ensure his income was as steady as his hours.

His own childhood had been ragged, broken and full of scars. After his parents' deaths, his grandparents loved him, but their love was tainted by grief and he always knew he was a daily reminder of all they had lost. He was the one left over. They gave him what they had left to give, and it was more than he ever asked for, although not by all that much.

Tom's grief needed to be cauterised by good, if dangerous, deeds. He had sought distraction and found it at first in sporting teams then in perilous sports like hang-gliding, then eventually at Duntroon. In the years post-Helen, he found it by risking his life as his father had done. Did he not hallucinate one smoke-filled morning at the edge of a burning mountaintop that he saw his father? Did he not seek out risk in the beds of beautiful women?

47

At ten-thirty there was a knock on the door and a waiter wheeled in a bottle of Kauffman Vintage Vodka immersed in ice. A card around the neck of the bottle simply read "gift".

The concierge called up to his room some ten minutes later, asking him if he knew a woman named AG. Tom paused for a moment and asked the concierge what the woman was wearing. He replied that she was wearing a fur coat which, to his trained eye, looked like fox and was undoubtedly real. The concierge added that the woman did not want to go via reception so, if Mr Stiles was happy for her to come up, he would bring her himself.

"It would be my honour to be in her divine company for another few minutes," the concierge said.

When Anna entered the room her fox fur coat dropped to the floor, revealing a black satin corset and a thin black G-string. Nothing else. She had the body of a belly dancer—all curves and suppleness, flesh and muscle. The corset fitted her tightly and was laced at the back. She drank a Kauffman while Tom unlaced it.

Over the next six hours Anna was his waif, his dominatrix, his wife, his mistress. They made love with a sweet dirtiness, circling around each other like a carousel, masked and unmasked in desire like a *carnivale*. They broke each other, became master and slave to each other. She was Natasha and Anna simultaneously, then neither, a spectre haunting his devastated but desiring body.

When he woke up, she was gone and so was his white tux shirt. He thought it may have been a dream, but his neck was bruised, and the jasmine scent of her body overpowered the vodka fumes in the room. Tom could barely move. He felt as sated and imperilled as an emperor of Rome. And he had twelve minutes before his meeting with Paul.

48

"Tom, over here, mate," Paul called above the din, waving one hand in the air.

"Morning, Paul. How are you today, mate?" Tom said, as a waiter hovered. "I'll have what he's having, thanks."

"Yes, sir, that will be the continental breakfast and a pot of tea?"

"Yeah, cheers." The waiter darted off with a brief bow.

"Tom, would you be interested in attending a few meetings with me this morning? Don't worry, you won't need to do anything, just accompany me, that's all. How about it?"

"Where?"

"Just around the corner from here, on Twenty-first Street. Two to three hours, tops, and then a joint meeting with the FBI and CIA. I promise it won't be a full day," Paul said, just as the waiter delivered two pots of tea.

Tom poured a cup of tea and as the steam cleared, he saw Anna sitting alone on the far side of the restaurant, eating breakfast. The waiter returned with two platefuls of eggs, bacon, sausages, and tomatoes. It was not what they'd ordered but Paul fell onto his plate like a starving man.

"Oh well, when temptation is staring up at you, you'd be a fool to ignore it. And I am supposed to be on a diet!"

"Couldn't agree more," Tom said, pushing the plate away, unable to take his eyes off Anna. *She even looks sexy eating a piece of toast*, he thought.

Paul continued with his tirade about who knew what, meeting who knew who, utterly unaware that he was no longer the centre of Tom's attention. Anna was wearing his white shirt beneath her fur coat. He watched as she got up from her table and slowly headed towards him, her stride purposeful, her hair moving as if she were in a movie.

As she walked past the back of his chair her fingers grazed his shoulder and without any other acknowledgement, she continued walking right out of the restaurant. Oblivious to the interaction, Paul shovelled half a tomato and a piece of sausage into his mouth.

Tom grabbed his napkin off his lap, let it fall to the table and took a deep breath before standing up and hastily excusing himself.

"I just remembered. I need to ring Vic! You know how it … oh, no, that's right, you don't have kids, do you? Well, I'd better not keep Vic waiting. I've got to go. Sorry!"

"Tom! What about the CIA meeting after breakfast?"

"Look, I've just got too much on today, okay? After dealing with Vic, I need to put a report together for the PM, you know. I'll be in my room most of the day, so you go ahead, and I'll catch up with you later."

"You can do that on the flight back!"

"Sorry, I need to go, I can't keep Vic waiting!" he called over his shoulder as he headed out the door.

"Tom, be in the lobby at twenty-one hundred, okay?" Paul shouted after him.

Tom managed to catch Anna just as the elevator doors opened.

"Are you following me, Mr Stiles?"

"My room now, Anna," Tom commanded as they both stepped into the elevator.

"I mustn't. I'm not supposed to see you until this evening, before your flight home, Mr Stiles."

"How did you know I was leaving tonight?"

"There's nothing I don't know about you."

"I get that a lot, it seems. Come to my room. Tell me your secrets."

As soon as the elevator door shut, they pounced on each other. In a second Tom had his fingers in her panties and took her index finger in his mouth, biting hard. Then the bell rang to alert them to their floor. They managed, just, to calm themselves and rearrange dishevelled clothing as the doors opened.

Once they entered Tom's room, Anna's fur coat dropped to the floor again.

49

Later, with Anna lying beside him, a vision of his daughters came into Tom's mind and he felt awake for the first time in days. He had done it again. He had bowed to lust and put his family second.

Knowing he had broken all his promises to himself, to Vic and the girls, to his unborn son, he felt sick to his stomach. And yet he put his arm on Anna's hip and reached over and kissed her slightly open mouth.

"I am trapped in my life, Tom," Anna said, with her eyes closed. Her hair had fallen over her face.

Tom remained silent.

"My father is a small-time criminal with ideas of grandeur. He is nothing more than a pimp, and if it were not for our mother, he would have pimped Tasha and I as well. If we had been born ugly, we would both be dead.

"Oh God, Tasha. I remember from a very young age our mother constantly being very frightened of him. But taking Tash to Australia with her didn't keep our mother safe from him. That's the kind of man he is."

She began to weep. Tom held her and felt Natasha standing

nearby, watching, despising them both. *Fucking on her grave,* Tom thought to himself, *that's what we have just been doing.*

"Diamonds. The package is in my room."

"The delivery?"

"Yes, I was to have seduced you, to buy your loyalty, to make sure I could get access to you at any time. We have been watched. We are being watched."

Tom thought of the surveillance equipment in the room. Someone had him on disc fucking Anna. But he was getting used to being watched.

"So, was any of this real, Anna?"

"More real than I ever wanted it to be."

"How can I save you?"

"Do this for me. Smuggle the package into Australia. They cannot be traced. I do not know the whole story and have not even seen the package unwrapped, but I was told they were diamonds—uncut and worth enough to arm a small country. There will be an exchange, they'll be used as barter; the diamonds must disappear. They will be dispersed all over the world."

"Why can't Vlad just have one of his henchmen smuggle them in?"

"Because the diamonds have been stolen from someone you do not steal from. His henchmen are all walking *Spanish*. My father has been over-ambitious. He thinks he is working for a higher cause. But he is just a pawn; I am just a pawn. And if the diamonds do not get traded, death for all of us will be the tax."

"Walking *Spanish*?"

"They have contracts out on them. They are all dead men. They have a week to live, each of them. They crossed a dangerous man."

"Who?"

"You do not speak his name, Tom, especially not to your lover. His name means death."

50

Late afternoon shadows filled the room. Tom stared at the family's characteristic black beauty spot on Anna's left cheek. He wrapped her tightly in his arms and tried not to think about the furthering complexity of the nightmare that was his life because the closer he looked the more complex it seemed to get.

Anna rose and went to the bathroom. Tom heard the shower run. He checked his phone. There were four messages from Paul, each one more frantic and angrier than the one before it, one from Vic and one from an unknown number.

Who fucks better?

"Might as well have knocked on the door and asked me in person, Vlad," Tom said out loud.

When Anna returned to the bedroom, she asked him why Vlad called him the Volunteer.

"I thought you knew everything about me?" Tom replied with a smirk.

"I know you fought fires but is it code for something else?"

"Not that I know of, but it seems what I know is becoming less and less by the day."

She lay over him and kissed him, long and deeply.

"Pick up the parcel at seven, downstairs. No talking, no drinks. This is goodbye."

"Stay another hour, Anna. Come back to bed."

"I wish you a happy life," she said and walked out the door.

The afternoon shadows lengthened and without Anna's presence the room felt cold. Tom's phone chimed—a new message from Paul.

Dinner at 8, be there, you bastard. What were you doing all day? You never left your room. FYI = Wheel up delayed.

51

Tom's worst fear was that Paul would pick up something up with his sixth sense which, according to Paul, he had become renowned for within the agency.

If he confessed to everything now, he might still be able to recruit Paul to assist him in getting rid of Vlad. He could just come clean about the whole business of affairs and extortion, resign from the taskforce and go back to his business.

People would recognise him at first but that would soon subside, and he would become another anonymous suit walking through revolving doors into merchant banks and insurance companies. The fraud guy. Well, he was a fraud, wasn't he? Then his life could go back to fraud investigations and spending more time with his kids. He could live a comfortable life with Vic and the girls and teach his son to ride a bike, make a slingshot, dribble a soccer ball.

They would holiday every year in the Greek Islands, in Helen's birthplace of Lindos in Rhodes. Perhaps he'd make more children with Vic. He saw himself barbequing line-caught fish for his grandchildren.

He knew he should call Vic, but he just couldn't do it. He had decided against becoming a Black Ops agent. All he really *had* to do was sort out Vlad.

He entered the bar and nodded to the barman. There was the same kind of crowd as the night before—congressmen, diplomats, ageing NBA players. Except tonight there was extra security. Conspicuous in their dark suits and sunglasses, two men dressed as Arabs, who Tom sensed were not Arabs at all, and three women in burqas, sat around a table eating nuts and drinking mineral water. Aretha Franklin was singing *R.E.S.P.E.C.T.* Tom saw Anna enter in the mirror of the bar. She caught his eye in the reflection.

She looked stunning with her hair freshly washed and blow-waved but she was dressed sedately in a blue suit and pants, with only her sequined heels hinting at her wild spirit. *She means business,* Tom thought.

Anna walked up to Tom, lifted his hand, and placed the parcel into his palm. Then she left. The two disguised as Arabs followed her out. The women dressed in dark floral burqas left via a different exit. Tom walked out into the street, saw the whole group load into a black stretch Hummer and drive off.

Tom went back inside, drank two Glenmorangies and then a third, feeling his heart deaden a little. He sensed Anna was in trouble and only he could save her. He at least owed it to Natasha, who he loved (he admitted that now), to deliver the parcel. Telling Paul was out of the question. He doubted Paul would care enough to save Anna.

His mind raced back over Natasha's death, Vlad's blackmail, the approach from the prime minister, Washington, Anna. He had gone from a simple backburn to the hottest spot on the planet. He had gone from a business and family man with a weakness for women to a running boy for the mafia, lover of dangerous half-sisters, special attaché to the prime minister, and potential killer.

His phone chimed twice.

I am waiting!?? P

52

"Thank you, Anthony. I'm ready to order now, please," said Paul sarcastically as soon as Tom was seated by the waiter.

"Very well, sir," the waiter replied as he took out his touchscreen tablet.

"I'll have the lobster tail for entrée, grilled Norwegian salmon with the fennel crust and Chardonnay butter sauce. And a bottle of Dog Point Sauvignon Blanc, thank you, Anthony."

"Hungry, Paul?" Tom said.

"You wasted seven more minutes of my time Tom, which is seven minutes less to brief you on what's coming up. You know what seven minutes means in this business?"

"Let me guess—the difference between life and death?"

"No, Tom, something much more important than that," Paul said and allowed a smile to break across his face.

The waiter bowed and turned to Tom, "And for you, sir?"

Tom was surprised that the waiter didn't look embarrassed or fazed by the snippet of conversation he had just heard. Tom guessed, in a city like Washington, any talk of espionage, like high finance or election campaigns, was normal dinner table chitchat. How many lives had been decided upon at just such a meeting?

How many democracies had been saved or consigned to a foolish president, how many dictators had had their fates blighted, between courses, at this very table? Tom ordered the steak frites and a Buffalo Trace, just for a change.

"Thank you, gentlemen. I will bring your drinks immediately," announced Anthony, as he deftly placed napkins on their laps.

Throughout dinner, Paul spoke in a code that Tom struggled to decipher. There was a BOZ in Washington, but Paul didn't know what bar he was playing at or who was paying the piper. Paul said his dance card was empty and had Tom changed his mind about dancing with the devil? Isn't that what he had been doing for a long time now? Tom grinned.

Paul asked for Tom's room access card so his belongings could be packed and taken to the car. Tom was to follow him to the vehicle after their meal, where they would be taken to the airport to head home. Tom said little, trying to digest Paul's cryptic conversation, God knows what he was agreeing to just by sending back the overcooked spinach!

Paul didn't really seem to be seeking conversation. He was content, between mouthfuls, to recite a monologue, spraying out code words to remind himself of what he needed to focus on. Tom was soon full of steak and words and bourbon. He contemplated again what he should do with the package—hand it to Paul, risk his family's lives and Anna's, or continue to conceal it, and, as planned, hand it over to the Chechens?

Paul was silent on the way to the airport. Henry, also muted, drove right up to the prime minister's jet in that same secured section of the airport and the usual crew lined up in front of the jet, each illuminated in turn as the car's headlights swept over them. Paul completely ignored them as they stood at attention and saluted him as he passed by.

53

The wheels were suddenly in motion and, after a few sharp turns, they were off the ground.

After about fifteen minutes, Tom caught a familiar scent coming from somewhere on the plane. He sniffed the air, and his mind went in search of an elusive memory, which he could see at the very edge of his mind, as if he were squinting at a small figure on the horizon. The smell was floury, sweet, and though Tom was sated his mouth began to water.

"What is that smell, Paul?" he asked.

"Scones."

"Seriously?"

"Yes, it's breakfast time for the crew. They have jam and scones when they've been away from home."

"It reminds me of my grandmother."

"Mine too."

Tom's grandparents had been good to him in what way they could and their tradition of scones on a Sunday and having a proper afternoon tea with the good china was something that he and Helen had done with their own children. Tom thought of how his grandparents would often listen to Tom's dramas that seemed so complicated to his childish brain, and they would offer simple wisdom to guide him forward—*Do well by your family; a penny saved is a penny earned; the truth makes problems go away.*

He didn't believe in all that all the time. Compromise was the way of any life and things had to be balanced. The truth of his affairs would devastate Victoria and the truth of what he'd gotten himself into now would risk her life. He could think of many instances when two wrongs made a right in the real, hard, factual world. His CO at Duntroon had asked him once if he would kill a child.

"No way," Tom had replied.

"What if you knew that child would grow up to be Hitler?"

Tom looked out the window, at the strips of cloud, then down at the blue expanse of sea, flecked by white waves.

Despite all that he had resolved, Tom said, "Paul, I have something to tell you."

Paul raised his hand to stop Tom talking any further. "I know everything, Tom."

54

Paul explained that when Black Ops: Zulu special unit had been devised by the man simply known as The Tailor, it had superseded the Blue Ops unit, which was limited to terrorist surveillance, insurgency and reporting potential threats to ASIO.

The Blue Ops agents had more powers than the police but fewer than ASIO. Nevertheless, the unit was well funded by multinationals, who had billions of reasons to keep society in an economic free flow. With the increase in terrorism around the world and the rise of fundamentalism, The Tailor, who was answerable only to the governor general and the newly created minister for security, had devised a twelve-point strategy to ensure terrorism never touched Australian shores. Black Ops was point four.

Black Ops men and women were never meant to be covert. They needed to have the credentials *to be invited to the dance*. The worldlier the figure, the better—the more recognisable the name and the more public the face, the more access that person would have inside security systems, boardrooms, embassies. Politicians, media stars, even one Olympian decathlete, were recruited to Black Ops. Black Ops had a saying—*Your sister is a cold arse killer*. It meant that the spook was the last person in the room you would expect.

Tom thought of that line from his favourite movie, *Miller's Crossing*—"Nobody knows anybody, not all that well."

Paul continued, "Every Black Ops agent is flawed."

"My flaw?" Tom asked nervously.

"Yesterday, Anna. Last month, Natasha, last year, Suzanne, year before that, Christine, before her, Rebecca …

"Vlad is a five-dollar pimp who runs a couple of nude bars in the Cross, in Sydney," said Paul. "He likes to think he is high class, and his men think they're working for some kind of criminal tsar. They're not the sharpest tools in the shed; nothing more than failed security guards or bad UFC fighters with imitation Glocks. But Black Ops discovered that Vlad has a minor connection, through blood, to a serious player who, among his many enterprises, runs arms for the Chechens."

"So where do I fit in?"

"When Black Ops did some digging on you, they found an in— Natasha. You've been on their radar since last year. A computer spat out your name along with two others who graduated from Duntroon in the same year.

"You were an honoured soldier after Afghanistan. Your volunteer work potentially gives you a great cover and you have also proven yourself in the world of finance and fraud. So, you were named as a possibility to join the prime minister's International Fraud Taskforce as the chairman. I made that appointment a formality as I knew you and trusted you. It didn't take much to persuade the ASIO director and the governor general that you're *Zulu* quality."

55

"And the women? What did the GG have to say about that? She is a mother of three, after all, a feminist to boot."

"The GG is a realist, Tom. She's seen more of life and has more skeletons in her closet than either of us!"

"Seriously?"

"Mate, when we showed her a picture of you and briefed her about your history—love life included—do you know what she said?"

"What?"

"That she'd do you herself if she was twenty years younger!"

Like a schoolboy, Tom felt himself blushing.

"Tom, where you put your penis is pretty irrelevant to national security for the moment. We know that you're essentially a family man and with ScamTell, you pretty much proved to the world that you couldn't be bought. How much were ScamTell offering for you to stay quiet?"

"Five million."

"Jesus! Look, we need you to deliver the diamonds. We need you to keep face with Vlad. We expect that the proceeds from the sales will go through hundreds of hands, thousands of banks and perhaps millions of accounts. But if they all end up with who we think they will … well, let's just say we'll have Zulus all over the motherfucker. We know it's not the diamonds the guy at the top wants. There's another ball play but we don't know what it is yet."

56

They knew Vlad would call soon enough, as soon as he'd established that Tom was *clean and single*. Of course, Tom was neither. Surveillance equipment had been installed in his house and into the attics of neighbours' houses weeks ago by men posing as anything from pest inspectors to insulation salesman. This had all occurred when Tom last met Vlad.

"You see, by just going about your life, Tom, volunteering, attending meetings with the PM, becoming chairman of the International Fraud Taskforce, and taking the trip to the US, you kept making our plans easier. Your family was never in danger and never will be. Hell, we even have Anna in safe keeping for the time being. We thought they might use her against you."

"What the ... how?"

"Did those two guys at the bar in Washington look like Arabs to you, Tom?"

Paul gave Tom a phone inserted with a tracking device and promised that if he ever hit one and hash on his keypad there'd be twelve agents at his side in less than twenty seconds. Paul advised Tom to make his usual calls, check his emails and just get on with life. Tom just needed to await the call, set up the meeting, hand over the parcel and go back to his life until Paul called him again. Simple.

Paul didn't even ask to see the parcel.

"I don't care if there are cookies in that parcel. We just want to see where the crumbs fall, pardon the awful pun. People are waiting for it, the kind of people we take an interest in. Just deliver the parcel, we'll do the follow-up and we'll have your back all day and all of the night."

"Kinks fan?"

"The early stuff."

Both men laughed and Paul started humming *Waterloo Sunset*.

57

The air was brisk, and the rainclouds looked like tattered flags. The sun was the colour of an open wound. Sydney did not have its best face on. On the tarmac, Tom climbed into his car.

"Hey, Henry!"

"Hey, Tom."

"Not impressed with this weather, Henry."

"Beyond my control mate. Straight home? And pick up tomorrow?"

"Yes, home, mate. Tomorrow we'll have to play by ear. You going home after dropping me off or do they work you twenty-four seven?"

"Always on call, Tom, but I get breaks, sometimes two weeks in a row, sometimes months."

"Must be hard on your wife."

"Only when I'm home, Tom," Henry said, smiling.

Henry remained quiet for the remainder of the drive. Rain began to beat down. He drove up to the house. The lights were on in every room and in the garage. *How many times have I reminded Vic about the cost of electricity,* Tom thought, then chided himself. Inside

Tom could hear his daughters singing songs from the animated version of *Madeline*.

58

Vic swept past him, a gas bill in her mouth and a bag of laundry in her arms, the cordless phone nestled between her shoulder and ear. She gave him a wink and continued talking while his daughters continued to sing and dance in the lounge room, oblivious to his entry.

Dressed in her housework tracksuit that was pink, linty, and worn, she walked barefoot, instructing Helen's mother over the phone.

"*Manoula*, it is Google, not giggle. Just go to the search tab and type in Lefkada. Yes, the west coast of Greece."

Vic joined him at the kitchen bench as he was going through his mail and gave him a peck on the cheek. She smelt of laundry detergent. She told him that Angelo and Sophia were in Melbourne visiting Angelo's brother, who was in hospital with a broken hip. He had fallen off a ladder while cleaning the drains.

Vic filled Tom in on how life had continued in his absence. She had kept all the open accounts in check, written briefing notes on new clients and attended to the girls for several days with none of his usual help. And she'd had Tom's car valeted after the repairs and collected his dry-cleaning.

"Good to see you're fine. Oh, before I forget, I accepted a free, six-month trial for pay TV. The credit card company offered it and it's already installed. We can watch documentaries together and the girls have access to the Looney Tunes channel."

Tom said thanks and texted a message to the florist to have twenty-four roses sent over within an hour. He kept waiting for Vic to ask about Washington, the president, the dinners and especially the blast, but she was intent on relating the recent histories of all their relations and friends—whose son got expelled, who got a new dog, the selling price of the house on Mordecai Road.

Tom imagined himself as Odysseus returned finally to his kingdom, full of stories of divinities and adventures, only to have to endure the village gossip.

His daughters rummaged in his bag to see if he had bought them home any presents. He reached into his bag and produced two tiny bottles of hotel shampoo, a shower hat, and a cake of soap.

"American Beauty Queen kits," he announced, sheepishly.

The girls disappeared into the bathroom giggling and arguing. Tom looked deeper in his bag and found a book; not one he owned. He pulled it out, *Selected Works* by Anton Chekhov. He opened it and found an inscription.

What fine weather today! Can't choose whether to drink tea or to hang myself—Chekhov. Regards, A.G.

He flicked through the book and noticed that pages had been ripped out.

"No time for gift shopping, hey, Tom?"

"No, sorry," Tom said, without making eye contact.

"I guessed as much. You know, we have a baby coming. You're going to have to be around more. And be a bit more attentive."

59

Vic was always blasé when Tom returned from a trip. He couldn't decide whether this time Vic knew he had been unfaithful through female intuition or if his guilt was making him misinterpret her behaviour.

It was usual for her to be somewhat preoccupied, more interested in listing all she had done in his absence than asking him about his trip. He suspected it was because, like every woman he had ever known, she kept a dialogue going with him when he was away, wanting to, or perhaps needing to, alert him to all the various occurrences during the day; intimacy built through routine, like most relationships.

Trust and love ticking away on the tiny clock hands of a shared life: washing up the breakfast dishes, the lunchtime errands, some wedding or weekend planning done over late afternoon coffees, the bottle of wine opened at six pm, the bath times, the bedtimes, the bodies relaxing into each other at midnight amidst sweet small talk, and the simple comfort of listening to each other breathe.

On occasion, he would wake at three in the morning and find himself asking who he was exactly and who owned the house in which he was sleeping. Or who owned the bed in which he woke.

He would dismiss it all as the dreams and insecurities of an orphan. And if he woke and found himself wandering through the house charged with adrenaline, still a mystery to himself, somewhat baffled by the two small sleeping faces lit by the nightlight and ventured down to the basement to work the speedball for an hour, or hit the road as if pursuing his real self through the suburban morning, was it in any way surprising?

Had he not woken one night, many years ago, to see a fireman hacking down his door with an axe, and the room filling with smoke. Had not heard his brother screaming in agony, in contrast to his parents' silence, or worse still, their absence. Wasn't he lifted up and carried through flames to find his brother on the lawn, burnt and broken but trying to rise from the stretcher to chase the disappearing ambulance? All those strangers, ghostly in the smoke. And the female neighbours crying, the men shaking their heads and turning their backs on the scene to find their own children staring awestruck as the roof came down. And that night wasn't the sky itself alight with starlight, weren't those sirens unending?

Tom broke from his reverie when Vic placed an ultrasound photo on his lap. *My son*, he thought to himself.

As if reading his mind, Vic's face softened, and she placed her palm on his cheek. "Our boy," she said.

"Daddy, are you still going to love us when the new baby comes?" Sophia, wide-eyed, asked.

"Will our first mummy get to meet the new baby?" asked Angela.

Tom cuddled his daughters. "Of course, I will still love you—nothing will stop me loving both of you." He had no words to answer their second question, so he just kissed them both. He stared back at the photo.

The doorbell rang and Tom rose to answer. He opened the door and found Henry standing on his doorstep holding a white box full of red roses.

"Moonlighting, Henry?"

"No one goes anywhere near your home without us knowing who, when and why. Your wife can't order two fried rice and the beef and black bean without us knowing the restaurant, tasting the food, making the delivery."

"That's very reassuring, Henry but it kind of kills the romance. And the appetite …"

"Yes, but it is what it is for now. Oh, and I think I spooked your florist, pardon the pun."

"Goodnight, Henry."

"Goodnight, Tom."

60

The notes Tom had made on the night of the State Dinner in Washington proved to be surprisingly coherent and, after a five-kilometre run, he spent most of the day writing a briefing paper for the prime minister. As a finishing touch Tom added a comment in the margin of the final page—*things look fucked*.

They did, for most of the world anyway. Australia would be fine for now due to its mineral riches but what if the world fell apart around them? Every dancer needed a partner.

The ever-approaching finale to China's boom meant all of Europe was going to take a hit. Europe, as far as Tom could foresee, was liable to civil unrest, mortgage collapse and the end of infrastructure. If he owned property in Brazil or Spain, he would be dumping it. He could see an avalanche coming but could not predict exactly when it would hit.

Tom's phone began to chime. It was one in the morning. He set his pen on record and plugged it into the headphones socket of his phone, then answered.

"Tom Stiles speaking."

"My friend! You have my package, yes?"

Tom's computer screen lit up as soon as Vlad spoke. *Just Paul here, mate,* the screen read.

"Yes, Vlad. And I have greetings from Anna."

Cool it buddy …

"Do not be fucking with me, Volunteer!" Vlad yelled.

"Okay, Vlad. I'm not fucking with you. Yes, I do have the package for you."

"This is good. Okay. Good, we are still friends! We meet tomorrow. We meet at four-thirty, same hotel."

"Yes, Vlad. I'll meet you at the Four Seasons tomorrow, and I will have the package."

"Good. Is good. But do not be fucking with me. This is first and final warning," he growled.

"Actually, this is the fifth."

"Fifth what?"

"Fifth warning."

WTF!!!! Tom, shut up.

"You fuck my daughters twenty times, yes Volunteer? First one daughter, now dead, then another daughter, now gone, vanished, puff of smoke. You volunteer or magician? You make my daughters disappear?"

Hang up, Tom.

"Like the four seasons, what goes around comes around I guess, Vlad."

"There is a saying I read, Volunteer, it is Australian, I think. It is title of a book, but the book was not written by who it says it was written by, like you are not who you say you are, hey? The saying is 'life is such'. Do you know it Stiles? Have you read the book?"

Hang up, Tom.

"I think you mean 'such is life', but no big deal … and no, I have never read the book, I like the sparseness of Chekov, do you read him?"

Is this a fucking reading group?

"I don't read Russian peasants. Tomorrow Four Seasons. Don't fuck with me."

"Six," Tom said, and hung up.
You're a dickhead, Tom.
Tom typed his reply—*life is such.*

61

THE MAN DIGGING AROUND THE BOTTOM OF THE TELEPHONE POLE was an agent. Yes, he wore a council uniform, but he had no idea how to use the shovel. The house across the road now featured a 'to lease' sign. It belonged to Tom's elderly neighbour, who at seventy-two, was not going anywhere. A surveillance team had installed equipment there. Every thirty minutes a donut van passed by. Every fifteen minutes a plumber drove by. As always, the local court sheriff's van made regular trips up and down their street. All was in place.

His immediate focus was to get to the meeting, deliver the package and get on with his life. Then he had to put all the affairs behind him and take all his memories of Helen, his parents and his brother and put them somewhere safe where the pain surrounding them could be contained. He would live a small, sweet life with his Victoria and three, yes, soon three children. Maybe he could drink less, stop smoking nostalgic cigarettes, and do some yoga and meditation. Perhaps that would help him lose some tension from his body.

At lunchtime, the girls asked to go to the local shopping centre for some of their favourite ice cream. Tom thought it would be good to spend some time with them after being away. Rain pelted down all the way there and as they neared the shopping centre a sea of immobile red lights lay ahead in the gloom.

Tom decided to avoid the car park and park on the street instead. The girls clutched Vic and Tom's hands as they walked towards *Pepe's Gelatissimo*, the only place in Sydney that did double-choc coated cones.

Vic and Tom chose Rocky Road ice cream with chocolate sauce and the girls chose their favourite—rainbow ice cream, sprinkled with Smarties. They then demanded a ride on the merry-go-round inside the mall, shaped like the Wiggles' big red car and though Tom despised the Wiggles, he relented.

As they rode, a girl dressed as *Alice in Wonderland* handed them balloons and Tom started as an ear-splitting scream came from Angela. The balloon string had slipped off her chubby wrist and her balloon had drifted aloft. Alice came over with another balloon.

Angela let out a whimper and demanded, "I need another ride Daddy 'cos I lost my balloon."

Tom was amused. He wondered if perhaps he gave them too much or gave in too quickly. Still, he put another coin into the slot and the damned Wiggles started singing again.

"Life with kids, Tom," Vic said, as if reading his mind. "Just go with the flow. I'll go on ahead with Soph while Angela's ride plays out."

So, the Wiggles kept singing.

When Tom walked out onto the street, conscious of daughter and her balloon, he saw his Victoria in the arms of a man in an Akubra hat.

62

Tom grabbed Angela in one arm and sprinted towards Vic.

"What the hell's happening?" he yelled.

The man in the Akubra put his palms up and outwards, as if surrendering.

Vic was sobbing. "I don't know! I don't know!"

"Tom, she's had a fright," said the man.

"Who the fuck are you? And what have you done to her?"

The man said nothing. He just took two paces back.

"Tom, she was standing right next to me. She was just here," Vic motioned to an absent space, "and all of a sudden, she was just screaming! And I looked around and saw her being carried away by a man in a black suit, and I … I couldn't see his face. Tom, all I could see is the back of him! And then this man appeared out of nowhere. He brought her back to me, Tom."

Tom crouched down in front of his youngest daughter. "Sophia, baby, are you okay?"

"I'm scared, Daddy."

"Tom …" Vic said.

"Vic, are you okay?"

"Tom, look, look at him, the man who helped us."

"I can't thank you enough for saving my daughter," Tom said. "Where's the prick now?"

"Driving around with three broken ribs, a broken nose and a key-identifying witness on his back."

"Oh God, thank you."

The man raised the brim of his hat and said, "We take care of our own, Tom."

He looked into the man's face and his mind started downloading information. He saw a blurred photo of this same man running and another of the café that had just been destroyed. He saw an old woman and he saw an image of a man in black suit, a man who he had never really seen, carrying away his daughter. Again, he saw the man who was now standing before him holding his wife. Then he saw a boy lying on the front lawn of a burning house.

"You can't be …" He paused, lost for words. "It's my brother. It's Terry."

Tom Stiles. Mind gone to blue screen … with no one tapping out messages.

63

Tom and Terry sat across from each other at their kitchen table, a bottle of whisky between them. They were speechless, just as they had been all the way home.

"After we both recovered from our minor burns in hospital our grandparents couldn't take the two of us and I was fostered out because I was the eldest. I moved from house to house, always given attention, always trying to get myself in trouble.

"When I was eighteen the state released me for the first time. I was so angry, self-absorbed. I always knew I could find you if I wanted to, but my anger was too deep. And I didn't want to spread it to you, to damage you with it.

"It's been five years since I finally had the courage to find you. But then Helen died, and I figured you needed time. I haven't had the guts to approach you. I just thought, why stuff up his life? Play dead for his sake. Geronimo, remember?"

"I remember," Tom said.

"I've always felt that, as your older brother, I should have protected you and you would hate me because I didn't. So, I found a job in your neighbourhood area working in the local courts as a sheriff's officer so I could keep you and your family in sight. Even though it was hard not talking to you, I guess it was important for me to see you on a regular basis. I was unable to protect you when we were kids so when I found you again, I made it my priority to keep you all safe."

Terry's story spun around the room.

Vic joined them, sitting beside Tom, her head on his shoulder. "My God, you two look alike."

"So that was you who saved Vic at the café?" Tom asked.

"Yes."

"How did you know that would happen?" Vic asked.

"It was a hunch. Things had been going on around that café for months, strange meetings, drop offs, but no way did I think it would be an old woman losing control of her car."

Apart from the bags under Terry's eyes and the light gray hair sprinkled through the dark, he was a mirror image of Tom. They were the same height and similar build, though Tom had a more muscular body from his weight training and morning runs. Their eyes were almost the same colour, with Terry's a deeper blue. "My God. I have my brother back."

He looked at Vic in disbelief and saw tears streaming down her face.

"My brother." He reached over and hugged Terry. They hugged for a long time. Tom felt breathless, somewhere between grief for all the years lost and elation for their future together.

"What about your own family, Terry. Are you married?" Vic asked.

"I was once, yes," Terry replied. "We didn't have any kids and it didn't last long. I was drinking back then. I was on the force, but I wasn't a nice person. I lost my job and she finally divorced me."

"How long were you married?"

"Four years but it was over in the second, she just hadn't the heart to leave me earlier. And when she finally did, that's when my drinking peaked and, after nineteen years on the force, I lost my job because of it. Then I really bottomed out, until one day I woke up in a rehab centre with no knowledge of how I'd gotten there.

"It took me six months to dry out and for the first time in ages, I started thinking straight. I knew it was too late for my marriage and career, but I was alive and finally had a clear head. I realised that I wanted, more than anything, to find Tom. It became my goal and it kept me focused and away from drinking. I took this job to be near you and I haven't had a drink since. That was five years ago."

Vic asked him about his job, and he explained that his role as a sheriff's officer was similar to that of a police officer but without full police powers. He said he performed general law enforcement duties within the local courts system and could serve and execute court orders and work the enforcement duties of the jury system.

"But let me ask you both something now," Terry said.

"Of course," Tom said.

"Why would anyone try to abduct Sophia?"

Tom and Vic looked like they had been slapped. In the emotion of finding Terry, they had forgotten they had almost lost their daughter.

Vlad, Tom thought. He checked the time. It was three-thirty.

64

Tom opened the door as the doorbell rang for the second time, and was shocked to see Paul, flanked by police officers and what appeared to be another two plain-clothes detectives behind him.

"Paul, what the fuck just happened? Has Vlad been tipped?"

"I came as soon as I heard. And I have no idea who you are talking about, Tom," Paul said, with a creased forehead and stern eyes. Then he urged the officers inside and pulled Tom out the door.

"Easy, boy," Paul said. "Keep your tongue in check. Those cops think I am here because of your attaché status and that what happened is because of your new profile. The police will take statements and it will be filed and investigated as per usual on level one. But I hate to tell you this, we suspect this is level five."

"I haven't got time for codes, Paul. Who tried to take my daughter?"

"We were there when it happened, Tom, and we got the guy. When it all kicked off, we were about to move in when your brother intervened. We backed off and then pursued the car as he tried to get away. By the way, where did your brother learn to punch like that? Anyway, the perpetrator has been apprehended."

"Who is he?"

"He's just a running boy. He's too smart to talk and too dumb to have much useful information but Blue Ops know who he works for."

"Who does he work for?"

"You need to keep your meeting. I'll fill you in on the way."

"Okay, I'll let Vic know. She's safe now, right?"

"Yes, the police will not stand down until we return. Come on, Tom. Grab the package and let's go. I've got a story for you, but in the car."

"Paul, I just found my brother, can't we delay this?"

"No, time is more important now than ever. Sorry, mate, but the police will take care of your family until we are back. Hustle time."

Both Vic and Terry encouraged him to go to his appointment. He promised he would be back soon.

65

Paul sat in front with Henry. Tom's rage simmered. He didn't trust himself. He was going to tear Vlad's face off. He was going to break his windpipe, then his nose. Then he was going to gouge out both his eyes.

If Paul thought Terry could punch, wait until he saw Tom take this motherfucking pimp-arsed coward apart. There'd be nothing left of him in the three minutes it would take the agents to arrive.

Neither Paul nor Henry spoke. Henry drove as if he was going to the library. He even stopped at red lights and pedestrian crossings. Now and again, Paul glanced at Tom.

"So, Paul, what's the story you were going to tell me?" Tom said.

"I'm waiting, mate."

"Waiting for what?"

"That pen I gave you monitors your blood pressure and heart rate. I need it to lower to your resting heartbeat of fifty-six bpm, which is very impressive by the way, and for your blood pressure to lower. I can't tell who's more stressed, you or Henry having to drive like a citizen!

"I need you focused for a chess game, not a street fight. This is a civilian interaction. The bartender will bring you a drink and you will drink it. Then call for another. You will not be meeting Vlad. Things have escalated. So, holster your gun. You hand over the parcel and foot it out of there. Now more than ever we need this to lock in place."

"What is going on, Paul? What has escalated? Why Sophia?"

"Henry, pull over here and go buy the most expensive woman's watch you can find in that jeweller. Just tell them to bill Mr Doehunter. And make sure the box is encrusted with diamonds."

"Yes, sir," said Henry and left. He locked the car doors.

"Tom, it seems that Vlad did actually love his daughters. We didn't see that coming. He's been trying to contact Anna night and day. We figured he just wanted to send her off to fuck some other asset, but we let her talk to him anyway and the poor bastard was in tears. He decided that you double-crossed Anna, got her kidnapped, and after he got his package he was going to try and trade your daughter for his."

"I will kill him. You must allow me to kill him."

"And ruin his stupid little plan? The police would have found him in fifteen minutes. He was going to use his black Merc with number plates Vlad 00 for the abduction. Idiot. Gormless fool told all this to Anna. You know she calls him Pa? That's hilarious, like *little house on the fucking prairie*!"

"So why didn't you stop all of this before it started? Why risk my little girl?"

"That's what I mean by escalated. It wasn't Vlad; his Merc was still three kilometres away when the attempted abduction happened. The architect of all of this wants to meet you. The failed abduction was planned to fail. We have been watching, listening; we think we have finally got him to show his face."

"Who?"

The driver's door opened, and Henry handed over the watch box and a bowie knife in a harness that strapped around the shoulders.

"You're about to meet him, mate. And right now, the less you know the better."

66

THE BARTENDER BROUGHT OVER THE DRINK. VLAD WAS NOWHERE TO be seen, as Paul had predicted. Tom's anger had reduced his observational skills. He couldn't identify who the players were in the bar. Everyone looked guilty and innocent at the same time.

Focus, Tom, he thought, *this isn't amateur hour at the Hillbilly Hotel anymore.* There could be trouble lurking in a pencil skirt or a cheap suit. Real criminals put their vanities aside. The girl flirting with the concierge looked like an escort. The concierge was new, but he was an old man with Italian gestures; safe. The bartender had been put in place by Paul, he knew that. But the dark-skinned guy with the goatee and the duffle coat eating a schnitzel, was he an assassin or an advertiser? And the young man holding a bag full of DVDs from JB Hi-Fi, was he a tourist or a terrorist?

Focus, for Christ's sake. He felt like slapping himself in the face. Instead, he downed his drink and called for another.

An old man holding a copy of *Paris Match*, with Brigitte Bardot on the cover, limped over, supporting himself on his cane and sat directly across from him. Once he was seated, he opened his magazine and started to read. The bartender brought him a coffee and the man tipped him ten dollars. Why no wait staff? *Stop being para-*

noid, he chided himself. *The place isn't busy. They don't need staff for off-peak times. Drop off and go,* he reminded himself.

The man opposite him was at least seventy years old and trim. *Perhaps he still walked every day and watched his diet,* Tom thought. *Perhaps he's an old college professor here for a conference at Sydney University.* He had clumps of white hair between bald spots, so he looked somewhat ill, like he had leukaemia. However, Tom recognised his condition as alopecia, a stress condition which affects the scalp and nothing else. His shoulders were broad beneath his suit.

The man put down the magazine and stared at Tom with cloudy eyes that seemed to have seen the world at its worst and taken mercy upon it.

"I am deeply sorry. I should have asked if this seat was taken, I do apologise. If you would like me to leave …"

"That's fine. You can stay until my guest arrives. I am expecting someone, but they seem to be running late."

"Ah, a woman, I see by the two packages. A woman's watch and something else, perhaps … Looking at you, my friend, with your lovely suit and let me guess, eight-hundred-dollar bespoke brogues made, I think, by the artisan cobbler who resides in Paddington, let me guess what the package contains."

"That is exactly where I bought my shoes! And at that price. You have a wonderful eye, my friend."

"Well-trained eye, perhaps. I am not a rich man, but it is only really the poor who can appreciate fine things, don't you agree? The rich are surrounded by so much finery. Give a washerwoman a horsehair wig and she will treasure it more than a princess treasures a stable of thoroughbreds."

"You seem to be doing okay, my friend. That magazine is no doubt a collector's item. The cover says 1964. Your suit is made of cashmere and the fancy head on your cane looks like silver to my eye."

"Yes, you are correct, well done. I own one or two valuable things which I appreciate and never neglect. If I allow myself one vanity, it is that I care for and cherish everything that belongs to me. I am a collector by trade but specialising in heraldry. A lost art;

heraldry and its history. But then I am old fashioned. I still believe a man can be defined by whether he polishes his shoes or not. But I covet little of what others possess. It makes the world simpler, don't you agree?"

"Yes, desire leads us all astray."

Tom was overcome by the feeling that he had entered the confession box. He called for another drink, the bartender brought it and the old man tipped him again, waving down his protests.

Tom asked if the man would join him and he agreed. Tom felt light-headed, swizzled. The old man seemed fatherly, willing to listen. Tom felt like simply stopping it all for a moment, his whole life, his whole being, just to sit and talk to this man and to say to this stranger that he had brought himself to this point stupidly but unwittingly. Perhaps the old professor was a counsellor, perhaps he had some wisdom in those merciful eyes.

Then Tom forced himself to quicken his mind. He looked up and down the bar to see if the new contact had arrived, but no one caught his eye or approached him. The adrenaline left his body. *I'm in civilian mode, it's okay*, he kept repeating inside his head.

It was three forty-five and if the drop had been postponed Paul would have texted. When he delivered the old man's drink Tom thought the bartender looked nervous, but he did not trust his mind. The shock of almost losing his daughter had thrown him. This was personal. Then finding his brother in the same moment. He was struggling to find the pattern again. Struggling to see the bigger picture. *People aren't numbers, they don't act in predictable ways.* With people there were no certainties, no stated values.

"You seem troubled, my friend. Is this a first date? Is she very beautiful?"

"No, no." Tom smiled. "It's just been a busy day and I'd like to go home."

"Of course. Life can get so chaotic sometimes."

"What is your name by the way?"

"Cerberus, just Cerberus, no surname, Mr Stiles."

"Tom is fine. Cerberus, oh I see, the head of your cane has three dogs' heads, teeth bared. Cerberus guarded the gates of hell if I remember correctly."

"A man of culture. You are correct. Some say he still does. You know your mythology. You must have spent a lot of time in libraries. Do you remember the figure of the Hydra?'

"The many-headed snake, cut off one head and two appear, from the Greek word for water, I think."

"Yes, very good. The world and its problems can be like that, Tom, kill one problem, two appear in its place."

"Have we met before? You know my name."

"You are a world figure, Tom, in all the papers. Maybe on the cover of *Paris Match* one day? No, we have not met. I move in much lower circles. My associates are certainly not of any known renown."

"You were going to guess what's in the package. Care to try?"

"A love token, no doubt. If I guess correctly will you give it to me?"

"I'm afraid I can't do that but believe me, I'd happily hand it over and get back to my family."

"A family? And here you are waiting for your beautiful date? I am surprised, Tom, a man in your position. Yes, I read you had two daughters, a partner, one brother, parents died in a house fire."

"You seem to know a lot about me."

"Just what is written in the papers. After all, Chechen terrorists do not get disarmed every day at the White House. It was world news."

I've been a fool, Tom thought to himself, as if he had just awoken from a hypnotist's couch. *All this time I've been waiting for my opponent to arrive while he has already played four moves.*

67

In a game of chess there's a moment when your opponent realises you've decoded the strategy they were employing. They see it in a flicker, a half-smile or the most obvious giveaway of all, a side glance to the middle distance. The opponent feels something close to annoyance, as if they didn't want to waste their superior plan B on you and continue dismantling your defence, pawn, rook, and king. Cerberus saw Tom glance to one side and decided to call check.

"Mr Stiles, your next question to me will be how do I know you have a brother when you only just found out yourself. You will whine like a little child about it not being in the papers, etc. while your idiot friend Mr Henderson sits listening.

"This is becoming tiresome. Did you not graduate from Duntroon with the Queen's Medal? Did they not teach you Machiavelli and the mistakes made by generals? Please hand over the package and I believe the watch is a gift for my wife from the director.

"Cerberus is my real name. You see, I do guard the underworld and I do work for the devil. Now, Mr Stiles I have brought you and Mr Henderson up to speed and I wish I could have nothing further to do with you but, sadly, that is not to be. I bid you farewell for this moment. At some time in the future, I imagine I will have to kill you because the devil owned a tapestry business that you ruined but for now, you may live.

"Oh, and one final thing, in the world I move in, my superior does not need to listen to my conversations or have me taped fucking a beautiful woman. No, that is for children. My superior simply knows I will do as he has willed me to do. Good day."

Wordlessly, Tom handed the package over, feeling as small as a schoolboy who had just been embarrassed by his teacher in front of the whole class. Cerberus took the package and left the bar.

68

As if in a dream, Tom walked out of the bar and into the grey Sydney rain. *It's over now*, he thought as he walked, *they have what they want.*

He imagined spending the evening with Terry. He could unburden himself and tell Terry everything.

"I've dishonoured her and myself and I'm totally ashamed. I don't want to lose her or my girls. I will do anything to make sure I don't lose my family."

"Do you still love Vic?" Terry would reply.

"Yes, with all my heart!"

"Good. Look, I lost my wife and my job because of my self-absorbed ways. You need to ask yourself are you going to cheat on her again. Isn't that what got you into all the trouble with this Vlad guy?"

Tom felt relieved just thinking about it. There was a lifetime to catch up on. He hoped the cellar was still well stocked.

Henry screeched up onto the kerb beside him. As he entered the car, Tom saw from Paul's face that the next few hours would not be filled with nostalgia or be spent with Terry making up for lost time. Nor was it the time for confessions.

"Henry, we need to get to Tom's house in sixty seconds negative."

Paul started texting madly on one phone while talking on another.

"Three, no four, and I want seven units; the suburb is going to turn into Armageddon."

"Paul, what suburb are you talking about?"

"Tom, I need you to let me handle this just for two more—"

The glove box began to ring.

"Oh, fuck," Henry said.

"Oh, fuck me," Paul said.

Paul turned to Tom and mouthed the words, "Say nothing." He opened the glove box and took out a third phone.

"Yes, Director."

Paul seemed to shrink into his seat. He hung up and turned to Tom with tears in his eyes. Henry cut through parklands almost hitting two people walking their dogs and God knows how many ducks.

They reached Tom's street. There were police everywhere. Agents in dark suits. Snipers were positioned on every roof.

"Paul, what the hell is going on? Why are those snipers aiming at my house?"

69

A plain clothes detective rushed to the window of the car as it slowed down.

"Sir," he said to Paul. "Snipers can't get a clean shot. We've heard no gunfire yet. We got an anonymous text three minutes ago telling us to disarm and stand back."

It was only then that the detective noticed Tom.

"Just out of curiosity, just for my own peace of fucking mind, can you tell me how they got past twenty officers and into the house?" shouted Paul.

"They had the correct papers, with your signature on it, sir, all the green forms and duplicates. They had been in the house before. They're from the cable channel. Tom's wife also vouched for them."

"Cerberus. Shit."

"But he has the diamonds," Tom said.

"No, Tom, it turns out we didn't give him the diamonds. The Tailor called. We freed Anna after you made the delivery and she's now invisible. It looks like she double-crossed Vlad, but she would never double-cross Cerberus.

"We don't know who has the diamonds, but Vlad thinks you have them. Cerberus won't want them now, but he knows our operations back to front. We have termites, it seems. And he won't let you escape unpunished."

"Unpunished? Paul, listen to me, there are men in that house holding Vic, my children and brother hostage over diamonds it seems I never had. I don't care if they are working for a mafia boss or a mafia tsar, either way, things are not looking pretty. What the fuck do they want from me?"

"They want you to go inside alone but that can't happen," the detective said, reading a new text on his phone.

70

Tom jumped out of the car and sprinted to the front door of his home. Neither Paul nor Henry reacted fast enough to stop him. Some of the officers drew and aimed at him as he ran but then realised who he was.

The front door opened, and a silencer beckoned him in. The door closed behind him. A gun was pushed into his back and he was jostled forward. There was a splattering of blood on the carpet. Tom felt his knees buckle. Somewhere in the house nursery rhymes were playing. On the TV screen Brittany Spears was singing *Just Like a Circus*.

There's only two types of guys out there
Ones that can hang with me and ones that are scared
So baby, I hope that you came prepared
I run a tight ship so beware.

"I will do anything you ask. I beg you, don't hurt my family."

"Shut the fuck up."

"Tell me what you want?"

"Be quiet or we will kill you last, after you watch as we shoot your family between the eyes, one by one."

They're alive, Tom thought.

He led Tom through the kitchen where the bodies of the two police officers lay, a bullet through each of their eyes. *Just like Bell,* Tom thought.

The man walked Tom into the living room where his wife was handcuffed to their two daughters. They were on their knees and gagged. A captive trinity. Vic was bleeding from her mouth and nose. Her eyes said, *Save us.*

Terry lay prostrate on the ground; pistol whipped, Tom guessed. The man gestured with his gun for Tom to kneel down as well.

"Hands behind your head."

A second man in white overalls with a fox logo on his pocket held a pistol directly at Angela's little chest with one hand while he gripped Sophia's free arm with his other hand. The man behind Tom pushed him to the floor and held his gun to Tom's temple.

"I don't have the diamonds," Tom said.

"We don't want them anymore. You insulted Cerberus, not once but twice."

"I've never met him before today," Tom said.

"Who do you think was behind the Chechen you disarmed in Washington? It took Cerberus twelve years to get the diplomat into that room and you destroyed his plan and then had the hide to give him trinkets instead of his diamonds. Do you think he can go back to our boss and say he has failed? You should never have said no to ScamTell. They were offering you a life of freedom."

"What on earth does ScamTell have to do with this?"

"Who do you think ScamTell is a front for? Anyway, I have said enough."

"Then tell me what you want from me. Or kill me, I don't care, just let my family go."

"We are awaiting instructions."

"Why kill the officers? They had nothing to do with this."

"They were in the way."

"Killing is that easy for you?"

"You do not know our boss. We kill or we are killed," the man at Tom's side said.

"Cerberus is an old man."

"Cerberus is the devil's dog."

"Tell me what he wants. I have money, I have connections. All I want is my family safe. They are innocent in all this."

"We do not want to kill you. Yet. Your family is in a war, like all the people in the world are in a war and there is a bigger war coming. Innocence saves no one in a war. The world has to know who he is …"

"He?"

"The Leopard. Ask your friend Henderson. He knows him very well."

The kidnapper's phone buzzed. He read the message.

"That slut Anna Goesoff gave you a book in Washington. Something to remember her by, I guess."

Tom looked at Vic and then away. Vic started to cry. One of the kidnappers laughed.

"It's in my desk drawer. Under some bills and folders. Wrapped in brown paper."

71

THE MAN WITH THE GUN AT TOM'S HEAD LEFT THE ROOM. Tom glimpsed his defining features for the first time—a long red beard, red hair, and thick lashes. The other man was taller with black hair, strong through the shoulders, and large hands. They looked like failed boxers; probably bouncers who had upgraded through a series of small-time bashings, maybe a minor hit.

Whoever the devil was, he had them in thrall. Tom knew there was no way of escaping no matter the outcome. He hated himself for thinking in such stark terms of an outcome, but these men were not trifling wannabes like Vlad's assistant. They must have known when they arrived, they would likely die. Their guns were authentic SIG-pros. Their forged documents, covers and acting skills were enough to fool even trained agents. They looked the part and neither spoke with accents. Yes, the outcome was clear to Tom.

This was a suicide mission, like the bomber at the White House.

What man had the power to persuade men to die for him, other than God? And what did they want with the book if they weren't going to make it out alive?

Tom heard the red-haired man going through his drawers. He had twelve seconds at most. He saw a shadow at the window and figured some of the snipers had gotten closer. Terry moved slightly. Britney sang, "When I crack that whip, everybody gonna trip."

"What did you do to my brother?" Tom asked.

"He tried to resist. We had to make him not resist."

"Two on one, both of you armed. Brave."

"I am holding a gun to your daughter and you want to be smart?"

"Like to kill children, do you? Gutless little coward. You wouldn't survive two minutes without your weapons."

"And you are an ethical man who fucks other women and risks his family?"

Vic's eyes said, *Tom, stop.*

"My brother is waking up. Two on two now, mate."

"Guns make it four on two."

The black-haired man turned to look at Terry. In that instant Tom slipped the bowie knife from his back and kicked the gun from the kidnapper's hand. Terry scrambled for it and so did the kidnapper, but Tom caught him by his uniform, dragged him to his knees and slit a deep smile into his throat. The knife made it easy. The second kidnapper entered the room, firing his semi-automatic in an arc across the room. The windows exploded. Terry got off a couple of shots but then took a hit.

Tom used the dead man as a shield. Terry had hit the second kidnapper in his left arm and his neck, but he was rising to shoot again. Tom launched the knife at him. It trailed blood through the air and scythed into the man's neck. He looked Tom in the eye.

Snipers streamed into the room. Tom looked at Vic and his children. He heard a cracking sound somewhere, as if the timbre of his soul had just split and crashed to Earth. Everybody was dead. Without speaking, he walked over to the second kidnapper's lifeless body, withdrew the knife from his neck and sawed off his head. Then, darkness.

72

Tom opened his eyes and stared deeper and deeper into a sad, dark place that never ends.

No, God wouldn't do that again.

He stretched out, feeling for a pulse but there was nothing.

He sat up and looked across the room. Death surrounded him. Tears fell profusely.

No, God wouldn't do that again.

Tom stood up, and gently took off the straps releasing his daughters' little arms as his tears fell down on their lifeless bodies.

Tom yelled out to Vic to help him, but silence filled the room. And when Terry didn't reply, his knees buckled, and he fell alongside his children with a sense of complete hopelessness.

As he sat up still, holding on tightly to his daughters, he was puzzled about their skin, how grey and cold it had been. At first, he'd thought maybe his mind was playing a mean trick on him. But then he'd lifted their clothing off their little faces and saw those grey lips and lifeless eyes … Tom was jolted back to reality with unbelievable anguish.

Maybe it would have been different if he hadn't been alone when he woke up and found their tiny lifeless bodies. Maybe if

Helen had been there. But Helen had been dead for a while and now the rest of his family was dead.

Tom turned and looked around the lifeless room again but this time his heart split in two.

Taking both his daughters' little hands into his, he began to apologise to them both for his mistakes as tears continued to fall. He told them that he loved them both with all his heart and how proud he was of them. He loved them for their smiles and the way they jumped on him every time when he arrived home. He loved them how they took care of each other after their mother died. He loved them for the way they loved him.

Tom, who would never be the same. His pain had become almost visible, as if a piece of his body had been cut out. He now had lost himself, or at least the version of himself that was unscathed by tragedy—an innocent version who walked around in some parallel universe where his family was still alive, ignorant to the incredible fortune of an entirely alive family.

Sophia and Angela's big blue eyes commenced rapidly flashing in his mind, ever so brightly. Their loud laughter. They were the co-keepers of his life. Tom was supposed to walk them both down the aisle of matrimony. His children were supposed to walk alongside him longer than anyone else in this life. They were supposed to live much longer than him. Tom was rapidly going out of his mind.

His family was now his past and that's when he decided to have no future. He cried out to Helen for forgiveness.

Tom's screams echoed throughout the entire house.

73

Tom buried his daughters and his Vic one day, his brother the next.

Helen's parents had no more contact with him after the funerals. They neither consoled nor condemned him.

In the months that followed he made a daily trip to the graves of each of his dead family, his parents one day, his brother and wives the next, his daughters the day after that. He spent his days almost entirely in graveyards. At night, he drank. He would drink until he passed out, and when he woke, he would head for whichever graveyard was due to be visited according to his desolate schedule.

He was beyond grief. Daily he thought about killing himself but reasoned that death was a peace he didn't deserve. If he had believed in heaven and hell, suicide would have been his first and best option—his life was a living damnation now. There was no one to turn to. He might as well have taken his appointed place in hell. He had gone from being a good family man to a killer. Not just of other men, but a killer of his own flesh and blood. He wondered if had he been a killer all along.

74

"Mr Stiles, Agent Willis, sir. Good to meet you, sir. I'm sorry for your loss, I mean losses. How are you, sir?"

"Coping, Willis. Just coping."

"Of course, sir. Would you kindly follow me please, sir?"

Tom had finally agreed to the meeting with the Black Ops Unit just to stop them from contacting him. He felt like he had descended into a caldera. After the short hospital stay and for the first few weeks he was distracted by the funeral arrangements, being strong, being Tom Stiles. Each night was a drunken mess of guilt and suicidal thoughts, sleeplessness or poisoned sleep. It mattered little—there was nothing and no one to live for.

He saw their faces everywhere, smelt them everywhere, felt his betrayal of them in his marrow. One cold morning, he wrote a will and a suicide note—*Forgive me*. He drank almost the entire bottle of Glenmorangie sitting in his car in the garage listening to Vivaldi.

Then, near dusk, he stepped out of the car, feeling perfectly sober. He unlocked his weights box, lifted up the weights and took off the panel that concealed his arsenal. It was time to die. Inside the box, he found only a picture of Helen and a handwritten note from Terry—*Not on my watch you don't*. It woke him, sobered him.

The next morning, he started training again, sometimes three times a day, knocked the stuffing out of two heavyweight punching bags, paying for his sins in sweat and torn muscles.

He followed Willis into a tailor's shop. Suits lined every wall and a man with pins in his mouth nodded as Willis led them into a back room. The man had large blue eyes, whitish hair parted in the centre and large hands. One of his ears was missing, close-range medium-calibre shotgun wound, Tom guessed. *Dangerous business, this tailoring,* Tom thought.

An elevator door opened, and they entered. There were no buttons. The back wall of the elevator abruptly opened. Willis ushered him out and handed him a security pass.

"It's called a hard-pass, sir. It's yours. I rarely have access to this area."

"But I've never been here before."

He made no reply, just pointed Tom along a long, frosted glass corridor to a large empty foyer.

A woman entered the foyer from a side door, carrying a stylish thin dark tan leather briefcase. She wore a black woollen dress with knee-length leather boots. Her brown hair was pulled back into an elegant chignon. She was perhaps forty, forty-two, maybe.

"Mr Stiles, it's a pleasure to meet you. Thank you for accepting our invitation. I'm Commander Alexandria Tap. Please call me Alex."

"I'm here because I didn't have much choice. You guys rang me twice a week for the last six months. I thought I was meeting Paul?"

"He had a job to do for me in Malaysia this week. These are difficult times."

"He reports to you?"

"Yes, Mr Stiles, as I report to the director, who will be joining us shortly."

75

Three minutes later, the tailor Tom had seen downstairs, dressed now in a bespoke black suit and a paisley cravat, entered the room.

"Apologies Mr Stiles. Always one more email to check. You have met Commander Tap. I am the director of Black Ops. No name, just the director. Informally, I am called the Tailor. Please begin when you're ready, Commander."

"Thank you, sir. Tom, I have been fully briefed with your situation and as I've said before I'm sorry for your losses."

She tapped on a touchscreen embedded into the table and a transparent screen appeared in mid-air and shimmered. Then images of Tom from the age of twelve to a photo of him entering the tailor shop a few minutes ago crossed the screen as the commander read:

"Tom Stiles, born: Blaxland, New South Wales, Australia, 09/06/1966; current age: forty; weight: 89kg; height: 188cm; hair: black; aside from a burn mark on right hand from a house fire at age seven, no tattoos or body markings. Parents deceased in the same house fire; subsequently cared for by grandparents who are both now deceased. Brother Terry sustained minimum injury and was fostered out, also recently deceased; current family status: wife Helen Stiles deceased, partner Victoria May deceased, twin daughters Angela and Sophia Stiles deceased, and in-laws Angelo and Sophia Gotsas are in constant protective surveillance now living in Melbourne. In early 1984, enrolled in University of Sydney at age seventeen; graduated in economics, degree with honours; entered bank graduate program 1988, at age twenty-one …"

Tom saw his life pass before him—images from his wedding day, graduation ceremonies, photos of Terry and him in the garden with their father, his daughters, Vic—a scrolling screen of pain for Tom now, a man who felt disinherited from his past, who had dishonoured his own name, who had no reason to live. He tried to stop himself from weeping, but the tears were filling his eyes.

The commander continued, "Allocated specialist assignment within 'counterintelligence and explosives' division; CI proficient in collating evidence, prepares and disseminates CI reporting of force protection information to all echelons; conduct intelligence gathering operations on first seen ordnance and IEDs, support very import persons (VIP) missions for both Australia and US, ASIO, secret service, state department and other federal agencies …"

"I can't take this," Tom said, broken.

"Please hear her out, Tom," the director said calmly.

"Thank you, Director. Tom, we know you have previously rejected the invitation to become a BOZ agent. But I don't think you know some of the features and benefits of becoming an agent and certain new information might make you reconsider your position."

"Please don't waste your time," Tom said. "My life is simple. Contained. I'm not the Tom Stiles you just described there. I may look like him but I'm not him. He's gone—dead and buried."

"We understand that, Tom. Life has been difficult, and I'll be the first to admit that I let you down—we, the agency, let you down. But things have changed, Tom. The world has shifted on its axis."

"I realise that but I'm firm in my stance. My life is over. I have nothing to give anyone anymore. My family is dead, my daughters, my partner and unborn son, my brother—I've had my entire family taken from me twice. I am keeping myself alive only in the hope that one day I may have my full revenge."

"Director, may I suggest we take Tom out to lunch," Tap said. "We can explain things a bit more thoroughly and away from officialdom."

"Yes, Commander. This place must seem very strange to Tom. Tom? What do you say? At least sit with us for an hour?"

"You are a persistent lot, but my mind won't change over the cab sav."

76

They were seated in the rotating restaurant of Sydney Tower, surrounded by blonde wood and glass. The room was almost empty. In the elevator on the way up a camera had showed a view of the descending elevator which was crammed full of people.

The only other diners were an old Jewish couple, who the director greeted with, "Shalom," as they passed. The first course of duck crepes had been ordered and Alex explained that everything said at the table would be off the record. She said they were trusting Tom with information they felt he needed to know before he discounted their offer.

Tom sipped his wine and hardened his mind. The city of Sydney—the bridges, the ports, the freeways leading to the mountains—circled them. He sensed that the city, the world even, was being offered to him, but there was no way he was getting involved with them again. His life had been reduced to maintaining the memory of the dead. It fuelled his need for revenge. That was all he wanted now. And it was a job he wanted to do by himself. He had untangled conspiracies before, and he had been trained to kill. He needed no authority, he wanted no restrictions, no paperwork, no law. He wanted to be a law unto himself.

Tom didn't want to talk about himself anymore or why he should or should not join the Black Ops. So, to divert attention away from himself, he asked Alex how she had first become involved with the Black Ops Unit.

The director explained he had seen Alex representing her country as the judo team manager at the 2004 Olympics, seconded from the military, all for Queen and country he cited. It had coincided with the first briefings on establishing a Black Ops Unit to support the war on terror, held in Athens with the Australian prime minister and US president. The director's criteria for agents were: a well-known public face, elite athleticism, moral values, patriotism, and a high IQ. A quick search through ASIO files had told the director all he needed to know about Alex.

"I discovered that Alexandra Tap's record," he continued, "included Mensa graduate, Rhodes scholar, bronze medal in judo at the 1984 Olympic Games, gold medal at the 1986 Commonwealth Games, and a Bachelor of Economics and Masters of Psychology from Oxford University on full scholarship."

When the director recounted Alex's 1984 Olympic glory when she had floored her Korean opponent with a right-left combination that no human eye could see, it was game over. Tom was all ears.

Unfortunately for Tom, Alex and the director were not distracted for long.

"Since the PM signed off on this new covert initiative with the US, we have all been steadfast in making it happen. We currently have four covert BOZ agents activated—one in Europe, two in the Middle East and one in the Asia Pacific area. If you accept, you'll be the fifth covert active BOZ agent and will be attached to the US. You see, there's only one assigned to each of these locations," the director said.

Tom barely listened as the director talked of Zulu time significance to Black Ops, global positioning, the Navy Seal alliance, and tier one capabilities.

"BOZ Agents are unique and are selected accordingly," the commander chipped in.

Tom listened and recognised in himself a sense of allure towards her, a slight desire to be accepted by her that he found fascinating.

"They must have explicit prime ministerial and presidential endorsement. You see, authorisation is needed prior to a BOZ agent actually being chosen. Your action at the White House has given you that very prime ministerial and presidential approval. It's all signed off and authorised."

"You can't make me join, can you? I do have a choice?"

Alex looked at the director before answering. "No one can compel you to accept, Tom. You're not conscripted, and the onus is on you to volunteer your services for your country."

"You've got to be kidding me. I'm forty years old. You're got the wrong person, Commander. My answer then was no, and it remains no."

"Tom, here's the crux of the matter—you're right, you don't precisely meet all our criteria anymore after all you've been through. We're pursuing you for one reason. You meet one criterion no other potential agent could meet."

"Tom," said the director, "I might not look like it after all the stress of the last few years but I'm not much older than you. You studied biology at school, yes?"

"I did study it, yes."

"Do you remember the textbook we used in those days, *The Web of Life*?"

"I do, yes, certainly I do, not that I can remember what osmosis is now or what the insides of a frog look like."

"Nor me, Tom." The director smiled. "But that title has always intrigued me, the interconnectedness of all things. The patterns at the core of life. The butterfly effect, I think is the fashionable term now. Think of all the little threads that hold a suit together …

"Not long ago, you met a man named Cerberus, the man who was responsible for your partner's death, your children's deaths, and your brother's. You were probably meant to die that day, but you disabled their plan. They had come to get something from your house. They killed everyone you love."

"This is of little help or consolation, Director," Tom said.

"Tom, when you ruined ScamTell, you put back their plans by a decade. They still want their revenge. But they still seem to want something else from you and we don't know what it is."

The director pulled out a laptop from his briefcase. As the waiter refilled their wine glasses, the director whispered in his ear and the waiter went and asked the Jewish couple to leave. They glanced over their shoulders at him and he nodded back. The waiter waved at the kitchen and the chef saluted and left with his staff. *There goes my entrée,* Tom thought.

77

THE LAPTOP SCREEN FILLED WITH SMOKE AND AT THE EDGES, TOM saw flames shoot out.

When the smoke cleared, a warehouse that looked like it was at a port somewhere came into focus. It had obviously been blown up but there were no fire trucks or police or security guards. Tom sipped his wine.

A man in a red overcoat with a rifle strung over one shoulder came walking out of the smoke. He was holding something round in his hand that Tom couldn't make out. He was wearing a desert *shemagh* that covered his face and a French army peacoat.

The man came closer to view. His eyes came into focus—blue with large black eyebrows. Tom didn't recognise him.

Then he looked down at the man's hand. He was holding a decapitated head. Tom let out a low scream. "Oh, God!"

"The man holding the head of one of our agents is Cerberus' boss. The Leopard," said Alex.

"What does he want from me? And why haven't you killed him already?"

"We can't find him," said the director, "We've been searching the world with the help of the CIA and MI6. No one knows his real name, date of birth, nationality, or whereabouts.

"One Black Ops agent saw him in Geneva and an hour later someone spotted him in Istanbul. He is a fucking holograph. He's completely off the grid and never uses a mobile, or a computer. We don't know how he issues commands or keeps control. But his fingerprints are on everything we would define as modern day evil.

"And now Tom, he sends us this. This is his first ever direct communication, left on the dead agent's agency-issued equipment at the crime scene. No fingerprints. He wants us to come for him. Specifically, he's trying to flush you out, Tom. He wants you to come for him. We've had your house covered and we've kept you safe because we let you down, badly, once before. If you come back, we can kill this man. He's the devil."

"Why on Earth would I go back into the hellhole? Answer me; why would I do that?"

78

"Tom, we have a very strong suspicion that the reason ScamTell asked you to investigate them all those years ago was because they were being extorted by the Leopard. Those two young men had uncovered a source of internet scamming that was coming out of a Chechen address. We believe the product they were about to sell to the government had the ability to track the scammers right down to one computer and then follow its internet trail for years.

"But we think the Leopard got wind of this—think of it, Tom, all the scams in the world shut down, except the ones run by the Leopard. Both those guys were high performing coke addicts and the Leopard used this to extort and infiltrate them. Our information suggests they wanted to be discovered because if their government tender got through, they would have been puppets being played by the Leopard. They knew this, but the alternative was having all their good work disappear …

"But they knew your background as well as we did. By sacrificing themselves in that way they could stop the Leopard infiltrating the government. We don't know what price they paid. No one has seen or heard of them in years."

"This is what the Leopard does, Tom—he puts himself in positions to cause chaos," Commander Tap said. "That is his MO. And our own agency was not beyond the Leopard's reach. I'm sorry to also inform you that we had a leak internally—Paul Henderson."

"Not Paul, no way. You're out of your minds. He is one of the good guys. Had a leak? So, he is dead now because of you?"

"He was Tom, he was definitely one of the good guys," Commander Tap said, looking him in the eye. "But we all have a weakness. Think about it—Paul loved power. I doubt he ever forgave you for outstripping him at that job interview all those years ago. And when it looked like you might become the main security adviser to the PM or a possible attaché to the US, we think that want of power broke him. How did those men get into your house? Who could have given that order?"

Tom felt unhinged. In his mind he saw Paul taking him off to the meeting with Cereberus and remembered how much Cereberus knew about him and the organisation. Paul had never explained fully how the men got into the house. How did he always seem to know where Cerberus would be and if he'd known where he was, why didn't he just bring him in? *Fuck,* Tom thought, *Hendo helped kill my family.*

"But why would the Leopard kill him if he was a double agent?"

"He had served his purpose. As soon as the Leopard suspected we were becoming suspicious of Paul, he silenced him."

"The Leopard has unfinished business with you, though. We figure he must know you want revenge. You're itching at the back of his mind. You're a missing set piece in his game plan. Let him come to you; help us kill him."

"Director, with respect, no fucking deal. This is too much to absorb and I don't want to absorb it—I've seen too much in my life already and I have nothing to live for."

79

Tom hadn't driven far when a black Mercedes appeared behind him. It followed him through the city streets. He made three quick turns just to make sure he wasn't being paranoid. The car stayed on his tail. He sensed something familiar about it; some current was running through his synapses and he felt his body tensing.

Tom pushed his BMW hard and got onto the expressway, heading towards Newcastle. The Mercedes was still gaining though Tom had hit 170 kilometres per hour. *Nothing goes that fast,* he thought. He plugged down even harder and his X5-M hit 200, but the Mercedes kept pace.

"Ok, fuck it," Tom said. "Time to see the sights of Lane Cove, you bastards."

He hit the exit lane at 150 and swung over a barricade, slamming onto Lane Cove Road, swerving through the lanes of traffic. The Mercedes tried to cut him off, but he turned 180 degrees and accelerated into a university car park. The bells for vespers were chiming. The old sandstone buildings were disguised by shadows.

Tom stopped, took a revolver from his glove box, and shot in the air once. The students scattered, and the Mercedes roared straight at him. Security guards appeared along the university avenues, driving little golf buggies.

Tom knew the car would be bulletproof; no point wasting ammunition at the windscreen. He shot out one tyre and then the second. The Mercedes lost momentum but was still coming straight at him. A pistol appeared and the first bullet flicked passed his ear.

Tom sprinted straight at the car just as the doors opened and two bearded men jumped out. He put a bullet into each man's thick neck, and they dropped like stones.

Tom swung the driver's door fully open, gun poised, and peered into the car.

80

Tom pulled the hood off the woman. His breathing stopped. Her eyes were both blackened and blood leaked from her mouth. He calmed himself and lowered the gun.

He felt something inside himself wake for the first time since the day of his family's death. It was a pulse in him that seemed to run along a unique pattern of veins. He couldn't admit it yet, he couldn't unchain it. But he wanted to.

Police sirens roared in his ears. He re-focused, jumped into the driver's seat and started the car after gently securing Anna in the back seat. He drove straight at the incoming police, making them slide out of his way. *Think hard,* he said to himself, *think hard.* Whoever had just attacked him had been waiting for a clean moment. They were interested in him. Perhaps they just needed him erased as a possible threat? Or they thought he knew something that he didn't even know he knew? *Think it out,* Tom.

He lost the police and called Commander Tap.

"Tom, we are tracking you. Where are you heading?"

"Kings Cross; this bar I've been meaning to go to."

"Tom, be serious."

"I am serious. I might take Anna Goesoff back to meet her father."

Alex was silent for a moment. "You have Anna?"

"Yeah, call it a surprise present. Whose hired thugs just chased me?"

"The car was Vlad's, but we doubt he would do it. We think it was Cerberus but to be frank, we don't know why. He could have tried any other time. Unless … Tom, was there anything at all that the killers at your house might have revealed to you, maybe you did not notice it at the time, the smallest little thing?"

Tom hung up. As soon as he saw McRarr's Creek Road he turned onto it and headed towards the reserve. He swivelled around to check on Anna. Her bleeding had stopped but she was clearly in pain, which only served to make him more determined. He slowed his mind as he pulled into the reserve.

Upon stopping the car behind a clump of eucalypts he conducted a quick check on himself for injuries but only found the shoulder of his suit was covered in blood and his face wore a carnival half-mask of blood. After helping Anna from the car, he asked her to stand and hold her arms out, with her cuffed hands stretched apart and then shot away the chain between the manacles. She fell into his arms. They didn't speak. Tom held his phone behind her back and texted Commander Tap—*Send me a new Henry.*

The creek floated by beside them. A young family were strolling on the horizon and the sounds of a faraway soccer match reached them. Somewhere, someone was barbecuing sausages. Kookaburras were laughing. Flying foxes hung in the trees.

"What's happening, Anna? Take your time but just try and explain it to me. You're safe now. I can protect you."

But Anna was too terrified to speak. She looked at Tom as if he were a ghost standing before her. Tom held her close again.

81

Tom walked Anna to the water's edge. He bathed her face, then his own. She winced and let out tiny gasps of pain. He went to the glove box hoping for a first aid kit or bandages but found only used cartridges, blood splatter, cigarettes, and a flask of whisky. He sipped some and gave some to Anna, then lit two cigarettes.

"I am sorry, Tom. I am sorry I dragged you deeper into this."

"Anna, I made my bed."

But Anna shook her head. "The book, Tom. The book I gave you."

"The Chekhov?"

"Yes, they were going to trade me for it. I needed to give you something that you could use to bargain for my life. They were going to kill me today. I am of no further use to them, but I reminded them that I still knew where the book is and that you'd trade it back to them for me. They saw you leave your home. They followed you and they planned to force you off the road somewhere quiet and make their proposition. Their plans changed when they saw you talking to the director; something changed for them then. I don't know what."

"Who's behind this? What's so important about the book?"

His phone rang. Commander Tap informed him that she and a new driver were nine minutes away. Tom killed the call and turned to Anna. "You have eight minutes to tell me everything."

82

Anna had laid it out as best as she could. She had given Tom the book so she would have a bargaining chip. There were eight missing pages and Cerberus had those eight pages. But without the book itself, Cerberus could not fulfil the next part of the Leopard's plan.

Failure would mean death. It would mean death to Cerberus and death to anyone who stood in the way of the book's return. Anna thought the book might contain a code, but she didn't know for sure. Whatever it was, it had already cost the lives of at least a hundred men.

She did know that the group the Leopard ran comprised of terrorists who shared a hatred for democracy. They were the outcasts, the exiles, those expelled from their own national or religious movements for indiscretions or suspicion of wrongdoing or because their blood wasn't pure enough. Most were just soldiers of fortune. The Leopard didn't care who they were as long as they were loyal. All he needed was for them to unite under the one banner of hatred.

The genius of this open recruiting policy was that no one person knew the whole story or the Leopard's motives and, as his myth grew, so did his power. A missile is launched at Palestine, a village is burnt down in Afghanistan, an embassy is attacked in Syria and no one takes responsibility—that's a signature Leopard parry. Create mayhem by stealth. Disrupt and then feed on the disruption. Disruption equals opportunity. A thirsty man will give anything for water, so how do you make him thirstier?

And why the Leopard? What happens when the leopard comes near the village? The animals panic, the women and children hide and console themselves with stories, and the men go out, hoping to kill him. But all they find, if they even look in the right spot, is a trail of blood that ends with a carcass. The leopard is gone, and no one can even be sure it was a leopard. The stories grow. Who would not choose to eat with the leopard if that was the alternative?

Anna had no idea how the Leopard maintained his power or gave his commands, but Tom was formulating a theory. *In the modern age we're all linked by technology,* he thought, *and what happens if you eschew technology? No digital signature—no mobile phone, no internet usage, no birth certificate or school reports or driver's licence or passport. You never use a telephone or pay for a gas bill. You don't shop or appear in a public place.*

Once that's all erased or avoided how do you prove an identity? Isn't it easy enough to be homeless as well? Once you have erased yourself and have started to avoid technology you can become anyone, you simply steal identities. All you need is a credit card number and a date of birth. If you need to make one call per day, steal a new phone each day. Tap into your neighbour's network if you need to send an email. Or even better, employ a line of communication so redundant that it has been forgotten.

Can you hear jungle drums in a city under war or even a city at peak hour? No, not unless you are listening for it. One option was to use a schoolboy's code in the work of a famous author, one whose work can be found in every library in the world … but this book was a collector's item, and Cerberus was a collector.

83

Tom was gone when Commander Tap arrived at the reserve.

Finding Anna at the water's edge, she covered her shoulders with a blanket and cleaned the blood from around her mouth with an antiseptic wipe. Anna was shaking, so she injected her with a sedative. She snapped the lock on a soft blue bag and the bag instantly froze. The commander applied the cold pack to the bruises on Anna's face. Then her driver put Anna in the car and tore off through the reserve, leaving her on the riverbank.

The commander took out her phone, plugged in a set of headphones and typed a message to the director as she followed Tom's vehicle on the screen. He was four kilometres from Kings Cross.

———

Tom and Terry had been to Kings Cross as teenagers. It had a frightening reputation back then, full of small-time criminals and their gangland trolls, hookers, strippers, drugsters and drunken men looking for violence or sex or both.

To Tom now, it was all petty, slimy, and inconsequential. These little crims were as soft as down pillows and about as intimidating.

But as kids they had walked the main street with fear in their eyes and innocence draining out of them as they eyed the girls, glimpsed a hidden gun or knife, and observed the tough guys standing outside all-day nightclub doors with signs that read *Peep Show* and *Mud Wrestling Babes!*

As he drove, Tom spoke rapidly out loud to himself. He outlined threads in his head, sounding like a madman cast out of Babylon, seeing meaning and futility in all his recent past events.

84

Alexandra Tap sat in the pose of a meditating Buddha on the bank of the creek, her eyes closed but her earpiece fixed in place. A chopper hovered kilometres above, awaiting her instructions.

However, to a passer-by she would have looked simply like a corporate woman relieving the stress of her day by meditating amongst nature, away from emails and conference calls and stakeholder meetings. No one looking at her expensive clothes, her fair unblemished face and the dark tresses falling to her waist would have suspected her true vocation.

She listened to and recorded Tom's rant. Her mind was working in Zen Koans. She knew in her gut that Tom had revealed something, but the information was not fully illuminated. *Let it come,* she thought, and in her mind, she began to recite:

> *Enlightenment is like the moon reflected on the water.*
> *The moon does not get wet, nor is the water broken.*
> *Although its light is wide and great,*
> *The moon is reflected even in a puddle an inch wide.*
> *The whole moon and the entire sky*
> *Are reflected in one dewdrop on the grass.*

85

Tom walked down the main street, just as he had when he was a teenager. The two seven-foot-tall men standing outside *LapDogs* had their foreheads crossed and recrossed by pulsing neon. They handed Tom vouchers for free drinks at the bar. On a plaque above the door the licensee of the premises was named as Vlad Mikula.

There were only a few patrons present, congregated around an early show soundtracked by Lady Gaga. The girl on stage had the bored, surly look of a checkout chick. She gyrated around a pole and put her arse in men's faces without changing the expression on her face. Her G-string was lined with five-dollar notes.

He took his vouchers to the bar where a girl in a bikini served him a half glass of warm beer. A trail of bright red spots ran along the inside of her arm. Two other girls wearing G-strings and pasties, one black haired and one blonde, approached Tom.

"Army or navy?" the black-haired girl said.

"That obvious, is it?" Tom said.

"A girl sees things guys don't. But *she* keeps her mouth shut, don't worry. Fancy a private booth?"

"Sure," Tom said, and slapped a hundred dollars on the bar. "A bottle of your best whisky and three shot glasses please, sweetheart."

The bartender handed over the bottle and the glasses and turned her eyes up at the other girls. "Lucky bitches."

The girls led Tom to a private booth and pulled a red curtain around them. The black-haired girl filled each of the shot glasses with whisky and told them to down them. They then drank another shot.

"Vlad is a friend of mine," Tom said. "Can you pass on my compliments for his service?"

"Oh, sexy, we're far more interesting than Vlad," the girl giggled, straddling Tom. "And a girl does not do anything for free."

Tom pulled out his wallet and slipped a hundred dollar note into her G-string. He held her firmly by her arms and stared into her eyes. His expression was calm, but it said, *Do this now*.

"Tell Vlad that I have a book of short stories. Then both of you can leave."

He then retrieved a second hundred dollar note, which he gave the other girl.

"Go tell him now but leave the bottle."

86

THE RED CURTAIN OPENED, AND FOUR MEN ENTERED. THE TALLEST of them beckoned to Tom, smiling. He then turned out his hands in a gesture of peace and slapped himself around the chest and waist to indicate he was not armed.

He's got a gun tucked away in the back of his pants, Tom thought, *or if he's not armed then all the others are. And Vlad is dead.*

Tom rose and followed the men as they walked casually through the club. The music had stopped playing and the girl on the stage had disappeared. The patrons and girls wrapped in tablecloths were being ushered outside by the two bouncers.

Tom was led through a succession of lace curtains then along a maze of corridors decorated with vintage porn posters and past three black doors that read "$10 for 10 minutes" and into a vault. A steel door closed behind him.

Inside the vault sat Cerberus. Behind him was a wall-length tapestry, framed in gold, of a leopard attacking a doe. To his left the severed heads of Vlad and his right-hand man, Emin, sat in an esky of ice. Each head had one eye open and one eye closed.

"Welcome, Tom," said Cerberus as he poured drinks. He

motioned to a chair with the bottle. The four men remained behind Tom as he sat.

"I see someone did *fuck* with Vlad in the end," Tom said.

"Yes, such a coarse man; a pimp, a leech, a fool. Let me ask you, Tom, as a father yourself, of daughters no less, what kind of man whores his children?"

"Hard to imagine, I agree. But I'm hardly spotless. And you forget, I'm no longer a father."

"True, but that is in the past. Please relax, have a drink. We have no intention of disarming you or engaging on a violent level. I'll be quick as no doubt there are agents on their way to arrest me.

"Tom, I haven't forgotten that you intervened in the processes of ScamTell at a rather inopportune time and that you killed my two associates who visited your home. Then your house was made into a fortress which prevented me from getting my property back, and in turn, angered my employer. Yes, the director's guilt ate away at him, as he had failed, as he so often does, to honour his promise to keep your family safe and he did fortify your home.

"I am happy to make a gentlemen's agreement and assure you once my property is returned you will never be troubled again."

"You just tried to kill me."

"Not I; Vlad. He wanted you dead because the fool still thought you had his diamonds. He planned to kill you and then his daughter. He had told her they were to swap her for the book but that was never the plan. I simply want my property returned and once that arrangement is done, well, goodbye."

"Simple as that? Except do you think my government, or the American government would be happy for me to go ahead and hand over something of such value to you? Don't you think they've realised it's a code breaker?"

"A book of stories? A code? Tom, you have been through a lot. You are paranoid and you are mistaken. I am a collector of precious objects. It is simply business. The book is valuable only in monetary terms. Plus, I enjoy the work of Chekhov."

"And yet men are dying because of it."

"Dead men! What of it? Seriously, Tom, are you so naïve as to think a human life is worth anything? A ferry sinks in Malacca and four hundred die, a factory burns in Antigua, another two hundred dead, a car bomb goes off in Delhi, one hundred dead and untold injuries. You read the papers, and that was just last week.

"People die because of greed or some ideology every day. It is only the West that thinks an individual life is of value. Why should a book not cost lives? Religion does. And foreign policy is the world's biggest killer."

"Cerberus, you've murdered Vlad and his sidekick. It seems to me the book increases in value with every dead body."

"Tom, you are a resourceful man. Find a way to get the book to me. This is becoming tedious."

"Or you'll kill who? My brother? Then my daughters? My pregnant partner? You've done that anyway. The Leopard just needs to yawn and I'm dead."

"Tom, the Leopard does not kill children or women; that would do him little good. He is fundamentally a teacher, a healer. He is trying to correct a cancer in the world—the cancer of the West. We must make people see and then believe. Victoria's death, your brother's death, your children … they were your fault."

"My fault? Do you think I shot her?" Tom rose from his seat but a large hand on his shoulder soon ensured he sat back down.

"Tom, if it wasn't for your interfering brother and for your own rash acts that night, my men would have taken the book and escaped easily, and you would have been left in peace. Believe me or don't believe me; it matters little. You will bring me the book or the alternative now is hell on Earth."

"I am already in hell and I will kill the man who brought me here."

87

"I will go to your home and take back my property and I will take out your entire suburb if I need to—there'll be a gas leak or a fire or a succession of car bombs. The details of the process are boring but be assured that whatever method is used, it will be deadly effective, that I promise.

"Taking this path is not my first choice because, as I said, we do not like killing innocents and we are masked by our anonymity. We are devils with a thousand names and a thousand faces.

"But now as you have re-engaged with Black Ops, I see no choice but to offer a greater incentive for you to return the book. It is clear from what you have said that, without some firm persuasion, you would hand over the book to them, not me. I cannot allow that. Ask Commander Tap or the director if they can protect an entire suburb.

"As I said, this is becoming tiresome, so you may leave now. You will drive home and take the book to the airport at eleven-thirty tonight. You will drop the book in the bin near the Qantas information booth. The pilot of my plane will soon have it for me. We will leave the country and no one in your city will be harmed by us now or in the future. No one needs to know about this conversation or the transaction. You will tell the authorities that when you got here, I was gone.

"Now I hear Commander Tap's helicopter so I must leave. You can find your own way out. You are lucky, Mr Stiles, most men do not get to see me twice and live. So please make the necessary arrangements. I have dallied in Australia too long."

Again, Tom felt like he had been hypnotised by Cerberus. The sound of the helicopter penetrated his consciousness. And then he remembered the ultrasound photo of his son and the lifeless, blood-soaked bodies of Vic and his daughters. "Go fuck yourself, murderer."

"Then you will die, knowing that other innocents will die today as well."

The men behind him pinned him to the chair. Cerberus tore down the tapestry to reveal a door. He opened the door and strolled through it into a dark tunnel, his walking stick beating against the concrete, slow and rhythmic, like the beginning of jungle drums.

88

The man who had killed his family had just walked away and Tom had been deprived of vengeance.

A man had his hands on Tom's throat while another held him firm. He heard a knife being sharpened in long, slick sweeps.

Then he heard shouts out on the street. Commander Tap and reinforcements, he presumed. These men would need to kill him quickly. He struggled against the arms that pinned him against the chair.

Then something heavy hammered at the steel door. One man instantly fled into the tunnel. The others, distracted, started arguing in a language Tom couldn't understand. Tom leapt to his feet, swung around, and reached for their weapons. He managed to grab and draw an M9, but they reacted quickly and soon had him held up against the wall, arms clinched so the gun was aimed straight at the ceiling.

Tom kicked out but they were trained to subdue an assailant; Tom could feel it in their grips. In the end, a punch to his wrist released the gun. Another man approached with a blade—a scimitar—poised to strike. Tom managed to get a kick into the kneecap of the scimitar-wielding man, and he overbalanced, then fell like a badly constructed house of cards.

One of the screws in the door jamb gave way. The tall man turned to the door and when he turned back, Tom hit him with a right cross that cracked his jaw and put him down.

89

THE DOOR GAVE AND SIX SNIPERS RUSHED IN FOLLOWED BY Commander Tap, gun drawn. Three men lay on the floor. One with a knife in his neck, one out cold, the third gasping for air with his throat caved in. But no Tom.

―――

At top pace Tom could cover two hundred metres in less than twenty-five seconds. He sprinted down the tunnel, his recovered gun ready, and his mobile's torch lighting the way. The tunnel sloped up and curved twice and he estimated he would come out eventually through some abandoned shop front.

A slit of daylight shone from beneath a door. A broken padlock hung from a vertical steel handle. Tom pressed on the handle, pushed forward, and went out.

Ahead, in a lot, were sixty or so identical black Mercedes. The cars were moving steadily, all driven by male drivers of various nationalities dressed in black with black peaked hats. A man with a clipboard ticked off a man's name, handed him a cap, and the driver got into a car and drove off.

Tom knew these cars; they were omnipresent at Sydney Airport —not officially legal or illegal. The drivers would approach disembarking passengers, offering them a bargain price lift in a luxury vehicle. Every hour or so an airport announcer would advise travellers not to use these drivers. They were not sanctioned by the airport and were basically scabs, undercutting the real taxi companies, and often intimidating passengers.

Tom thought of two things Cerberus had said—car bombs and *hell on Earth*.

He turned his phone onto view and streamed what he was seeing to Commander Tap. The screen showed black Merc after black Merc, one after another, filing out onto the main street, heading east. Tom had a sense that Tap saw things laterally, as he did.

Cerberus would not attack the airport, even though the cars would be inconspicuous there. There was too much security to contend with and it was too obvious. Plus, he mentioned his pilot. No, Cerberus had specifically said *Tom's neighbours, Tom's family.*

But a line of black cars with swarthy looking drivers wasn't just going to waltz into Vaucluse and blow it up with so many agents there. Cerberus needed a little hole torn into the web …

"Mary, Mother of God," Tom said out loud.

He texted Tap: *Meet me at the corner church of my road.*

That was sudden, Tom. You hardly know me.

90

The man leading the funeral procession was dressed in a red suit tasselled with gold. He wore a tall black top hat and waved a baton as he walked. Behind him was a phalanx of trumpeters, each wearing a medal and ribbons. A long trail of black cars moved at walking pace behind them. The trumpeters played a New Orleans dirge and beside the hearse a small man tapped his walking stick in time to the music.

They moved slowly along Vaucluse Road and as they moved, one car at a time, every one hundred metres or so, pulled over and parked outside a neat, well-tended lawn with a driveway swept clean of leaves. Then the driver got out of the car, threw the keys back in and walked off. The procession streamed forward, losing a car at a time.

Vaucluse was a suburb of families with men who had good jobs and women who had taken time off from equally good careers to raise their children. Within ten minutes, the local school would ring its bell and kids would be coming home or dawdling at the milk bar or somewhere along their route home. Mothers would be returning from grocery shopping and school buses would be moving local teams to sports training.

By the time the funeral procession was only six cars from Tom's house, it was stopped by a policeman. The funeral conductor walked forward to meet him, holding out his hand. The officer shook his hand.

"*Gendarme, excusez-moi, I honnore mon pere, natal Orleans.* It is our ... our customary, *que c'est le bon mot? Une moment dans la rue. Une moment.*"

"I don't speak much French, sir. Are you asking if you can pass? I'll need to seek a clearance. Just wait, *une* moment, sir, and please stand back," the officer said.

He regarded the old man with his fancy cane and the trumpeters with their heads bowed. He held his phone to his ear, nodded, and hung up. Cerberus tapped the hearse three times with his cane. One of the trumpeters took a gun from his pocket and shot the policeman dead. A moment later, six blocks back, the first car bomb went off.

91

From the helicopter, Tom and Commander Tap could see the systematic explosions occur one hundred metres apart, every four minutes precisely, leading up to Tom's home. Tap had shut down the airport already and diverted forces there even though she suspected Tom's hunch was right.

"We're low on backup, Tom. Sorry."

"I see that. He just needed the second guess to be wrong and he knew it would be."

"Next move?"

"Drop me in."

"I can't do that. You're a civilian. I can't put you in."

Tom knew what he was about to say would change his life. But he also knew the awakened pulse inside him would never quieten. It would never cease until he had the blood of that murderer on his hands. Perhaps, for the first time, he acknowledged that he was motivated by the need to do to what he could, like his father had been. *No man can solve all the world's problems, but you can stop a fire hurting your neighbour's property. Do what you can; that's what volunteering is about.*

There was something else as well. He told himself that it wasn't so, but he felt it in his body—Tom was no longer a family man. His mind had cracked open to reveal an abyss. And he liked staring at the darkness. It gave him succour.

"Drop me on the roof of my house, Commander."

"I can't."

"BOZ agent Stiles requesting, Commander," he said and saluted.

Stiles swung down on a rope and landed on his roof. He removed four tiles and slid into his attic room, punching through the insulation. He descended into his home, the home he had built with Helen, which now seemed nothing other than a battlefield. He heard another bomb go off but felt assured that Tap would have stopped the children from leaving school and by now all agents would be engaged. There was a war going on outside his window.

He descended to his study and heard men enter the house. They were moving quickly from room to room—maybe six of them, maybe eight. It would only take a minute for them to reach him. He didn't have enough bullets to kill them all, but he still had two grenades.

He took the Chekhov from the bookcase and threw it into the garden. Tucking the gun back into his shoe, he went to his drawer and took out his Lucky Strikes and lighter. He filled the lighter with lighter fluid, lit a cigarette and surveyed the room. He took a pile of books from his desk and threw them behind the bookshelf. He put the lighter, the cigarette case and the lighter fluid in his pocket.

The men had been through the bedrooms and the lounge. They were one room away.

92

Gunfire was being exchanged on the street as if the city had fallen into civil war. The few people still at home—retirees and the unfortunates who had taken an RDO, had been contacted in time and were now hiding behind the thick brick walls of their houses, under beds, in closets or at the furthest part of their large backyards. The whole suburb and its surrounding suburbs had been shut down. Everything was shut down—electricity, gas, and water.

Schools had kept their children indoors and were surrounded by police. The army was arriving in waves. It had taken the director one call to achieve this—one call to the Keep. This call didn't go to one person. He didn't even have to say anything. Tap had alerted all authorities and all the director had to do was call the Deadline direct from his mobile and the Black Ops Keepers went to work. They had the power and authority to shut down the entire country if need be.

Still, the dead lay everywhere. House fronts had been blown in and the injured couldn't be reached as yet, due to the fighting. Streets were aflame. Trumpeters lay dead in the street and a few snipers and other agents had taken hits. Some of the funeral procession had deserted as soon as the policeman was shot but the remainder had found good cover and were keeping the agents engaged.

Hovering above the battle scene, Commander Tap was issuing orders. The chopper was sustaining groundfire but she ordered that it stay in a steady hover.

When she saw an army unit stream in, followed by emergency evacuation teams and army ambulances, she ordered the chopper back to the Stiles' house.

93

Stiles walked out of his study with his arms raised and a cigarette in his mouth. Four guns were trained on him. He was pushed into the lounge room where Cerberus was sitting, hunched forward over his cane. "You have a lovely home, Tom."

"I'm glad you like it."

"Such a pity about all this, Tom. Such a pity. Where's the book?"

"The book is in the study."

"Go get it," Cerberus ordered. "You can lower your hands, Tom. Have another cigarette."

"Tell me, before you kill me. What's the real value of the book?"

"Child's play, Tom. A simple code contained in the most powerful technology in the world—a book. That code can be reconstructed a million times. I simply place the torn pages at certain sections, and I receive my instructions, my new identity, and the names of my accomplices. But the code only works with that particular edition, that particular translation. Only six were ever printed, only two still exist.

"You see, Tom, that edition was a misprint. It was a mistake, and production was stopped immediately. The world's security searches on the net, on mobile phone records, and uses surveillance and phone taps, all the while second-guessing what technology the mastermind has invented to become invisible in the world. No one thinks of looking in a book. A useless book; a mistake.

"A man in a public library with a pencil has kept the entire world in his thrall. He does not need to resort to YouTube! I read this once—limitation makes for power. The strength of the genie comes from him being confined to a bottle."

"I think I've heard that before. He'll be found eventually."

"Really? You remember playing hide and seek as a child? There is an effective trick in that game—move to where the searcher last searched for you."

One of Cerberus' men came in and said they couldn't find the book. Cerberus took what looked like a Colt out of his pocket and aimed it at him.

"Be quick about it, Tom, and I will kill you quickly."

"Hide and seek, Cerberus. Anyway, the longer I delay the longer I live."

Cerberus fired into Tom's foot. Tom bit his tongue. He concentrated, slowed his heart rate down, mastered his breathing. *Take the pain*, he thought. "One more cigarette?"

"Certainly, but you are losing blood quickly, so have it; tell me the exact location and then I will kill you with one bullet instead of twelve."

"The book is behind the bookshelf. Just pull it forward. It's very heavy. You'll need everyone to move it."

Stiles smoked his cigarette. There was no longer any gunfire outside, just the sound of a chopper and sirens. Stiles exhaled a final stream of smoke. He then threw the cigarette onto the carpet. A small line of fire raced along it, through the hallway behind the bookshelf, along the trail of lighter fluid he had left in his wake when he surrendered. Cerberus watched it, mesmerised. First one book caught fire, then another. Cerberus turned to look at Stiles. Stiles shot him in the head twice. Then the grenades went off.

94

"Commander, you have three months to get him fully operational and classified as a BOZ agent, do you understand me? I want him ready."

"Yes, sir. I understand the pressure you're under. I'll make it my priority."

The director shook his hand and left the room.

"Sorry, Tom. Straight back to work, I'm afraid. How are your wounds?"

"All good, healing well. And in case I didn't say it, thanks for helping me out of there. I wasn't exactly at top speed."

"Line of duty stuff, Tom. Any soldier would have done the same. Though I need to work on my descent a bit!"

"Tell me, before working for the director, what else did you do?"

"I did my officer training covertly while I was competing in judo. I was with the Royal Marines based in Lympstone, Devon, in the UK for over a year, then a few years with NATO strategic command headquarters in the US. Then back in the UK, working for both MI5 and MI6. The military has been my life.

"The director recruited me for this job while in Athens in 2004.

He surprised me with this offer. You know, I don't know if it was coincidental that he bumped into me at that time still to this day."

"Very impressive, Commander."

"Anything else you need to know?"

"Yes, how does the hard-pass work?"

"Down to business, then. Your hard pass, like every pass holder's, has been uploaded with your fingerprint specifications. The sensors on the pass will try to match the imprint of the user at the time of the actual swipe. So, if the user's fingerprints don't match the hard-pass specifications, it won't work."

"Thank you, Commander." Stiles nodded.

"Anything else you need to discuss? And please, call me Alex."

"Look, Alex, to prepare properly for the first job I feel I need professional counselling. I need help."

"Tell me why."

"Well, you know about my Victoria, my daughters, and my brother. But only Paul knew about Vic being pregnant. We were expecting a son. If I don't get help, I don't know what I'll end up doing before I destroy myself. All this happened, and I'm still alive."

"I'll get you all the professional guidance you need. Once a day for three weeks then we will see how you go. We have three months, Tom. I am deeply, deeply sorry for your losses. I know it's not the same, but you're part of the **BOZ** family now. We take care of our own."

95

A piercing red light cut through the darkness one Friday morning, hours before daybreak, three months later. One man sat alone in the cargo bay of an RAAF Boeing C-17 Globemaster at 31,000 metres.

Operation *Pivotal Velocity* was in motion. They were flying over the Straits of Florida in the Gulf of Mexico and the drop zone would be over eight kilometres off the coast of Cuba, near the remote peninsula town of La Boca.

Zero-three hundred. Dressed in a high-altitude jumpsuit with an oxygen sealed helmet, Stiles was ready to jump. He had done forty minutes of breathing 100% oxygen in order to flush nitrogen from his bloodstream. He was thirty-one kilometres above the Earth's surface, with a face temperature of minus forty-five degrees Celsius. He went over the jump procedure in his mind—free-fall until terminal velocity, then deploy parachute at a level of not less than one thousand metres.

"Whisky, foxtrot, hotel—Zero Ten Delta to base, come in base. Over."

"Base to whisky, foxtrot, hotel—Zero Ten delta coming in loud and clear. Over." Stiles recognised Commander Tap's voice even through the distorted transmission.

"Base, this is whisky, foxtrot, hotel—Zero Ten Delta requesting permission to deliver Big Bird. Over."

"Whisky, foxtrot, hotel—Zero, Ten Delta, this is base, that's a green light to deliver Big Bird, copy. Over."

Tom glanced around the cargo bay, gave a quick nod to the Loadmaster, and edged towards the open rear end of the C-17. The red light above the edge of the drop-door flashed.

Stiles looked down, his pulse echoing in his helmet. The sea was down there somewhere below in the black of night. He thought of his wife, his daughters, Victoria, and Terry. He thought of his parents. He thought of Natasha.

The root of all that hurt was still out there. When Tom had put two bullets in Cerberus' head, he'd killed the monkey, not the organ grinder. The Leopard was what Stiles wanted now All he wanted. He was hungry for the kill.

Stiles switched his attention to Commander Tap and his first assignment. The light went green and Tom Stiles plunged headlong into the darkness …

Dear reader,

We hope you enjoyed reading *Black Ops: Zulu*. Please take a moment to leave a review, even if it's a short one. Your opinion is important to us.

Discover more books by Arthur Bozikas at https://www.nextchapter.pub/authors/arthur-bozikas

Want to know when one of our books is free or discounted? Join the newsletter at http://eepurl.com/bqqB3H

Best regards,

Arthur Bozikas and the Next Chapter Team

You might also like:
The Book Glasses by Arthur Bozikas

To read the first chapter for free, please head to:
https://www.nextchapter.pub/books/the-book-glasses

Lightning Source UK Ltd.
Milton Keynes UK
UKHW011831050321
379874UK00001B/232